I0673799

Wakefield Press

# GUS AND THE MISSING BOY

Troy Hunter is an adult and YA fiction writer whose short stories have appeared in a variety of publications and journals. He lives in Melbourne and works as a marketing and communications consultant. *Gus and the Missing Boy* is Troy Hunter's first novel.

troyhunterwriter.com

# Praise for *Gus and the Missing Boy*

'Page-turning mystery fun that is meta-AF, full of wit and self-discovery. Loved it!'

—**R.W.R. McDonald**, author of *The Nancys* series

'*Gus and the Missing Boy* takes whodunnit stories up a notch, weaving the core tenets of young adult books in with the tropes of a detective novel, creating a great story that examines the mysteries of identity, family and friendship.'

—**Michael Earp**, author and editor of *Everything Under the Moon: Fairy Tales in a Queerer Light* (2023) and *Kindred: 12 Queer #LoveOzYA Stories* (2019)

'*Gus and the Missing Boy* brilliantly combines a twisty detective mystery with a moving coming-of-age message about found family and finding yourself. Troy Hunter's prose crackles with sharp wit and youthful energy. A fantastic book that skilfully blends humour and heart with a plot so pacey I didn't want to stop reading – I devoured it in a single day.'

—**Holden Sheppard**, author of *The Brink* (2022) and *Invisible Boys* (2019)

'This book made me late to a party. I know "I couldn't put it down" is a cliche, but I don't care – I couldn't put it down. A gripping mystery, told with compassion and authenticity.'

—**Amie Kaufman**, author of the *Aurora Cycles* and *The Isles of the Gods* series, and co-author of *The Illuminae Files* series

# GUS AND THE MISSING BOY

## TROY HUNTER

Wakefield
Press

Wakefield Press
16 Rose Street
Mile End
South Australia 5031
www.wakefieldpress.com.au

First published 2024
Reprinted 2025

Cover designed by Josh Durham, Design by Committee
Edited by Maddy Sexton, Wakefield Press
Text designed and typeset by Jesse Pollard, Wakefield Press

ISBN 978 1 92304 230 8

NATIONAL
LIBRARY
OF AUSTRALIA

A catalogue record for this
book is available from the
National Library of Australia

Dedicated to the memories of Ira Hunter, Stan Hunter, Kay Rogers, and Guy Stewart.

# Contents

This book was written on the unceded lands of the Wurundjeri people of the Kulin Nation. The author acknowledges the Traditional Owners and custodians of the lands on which he works, and pays his respect to Elders past and present, as well as to any Indigenous Australians reading this book.

# Prologue

*Today I became a detective.*

*I've always wanted to be a detective. Like, since I was a kid. I wanted to solve crimes, be the guy who's one step ahead of the criminals. I've always liked mysteries, clues, confessions, disguises, red herrings . . . all that stuff. I read loads of crime books, watch crime movies, listen to true crime podcasts, and trawl through unsolved case websites. All in the name of research, getting me ready to join the police force one day.*

*But I never thought I'd become a detective before I turned sixteen, two years before I can even sit the police entrance exam.*

*Like, you get up one day, go to school, hang out with a friend . . . but then the day changes direction in a heartbeat. My life is like a photo that suddenly went from washed out nothing to shocking colour. My world's tipping off its axis and it's all I can do to hold on to the skin of my old life.*

*So today I became a detective because I uncovered a crime.*

*And not just any crime, but a kidnapping.*

*And not just any kidnapping, but maybe my own.*

# Chapter 1

# Snakeskins

My phone's alarm goes off on my bedside table, blaring like an air raid siren. I snooze it and roll back under my doona. I want to go back to sleep.

Then I hear Mum yelling from down the hall. 'Gus, get up. I need help with these bloody things.'

*Argh, my life sucks.*

I drag myself up, knocking over a few unread books stacked next to my bed, and head to the bathroom. Like every other day I look in the unforgiving full-length mirror with disappointment. Still fat. *Doctor Who* T-shirt clinging to my stomach, my weird square-shaped face, and my untameable thick brown hair. No matter what I do, my hair still points out at strange angles like I've been hit by lightning. Having it cut short just makes my head look like even bigger. Once, when she was drunk, Mum tried to cut it. Bad idea. I had to wear a baseball cap all day till we could find a hairdresser to get it fixed.

'GUSSY!'

*Yes, alright, I'm coming. Don't tell the moon.*

Giving up on my hair, I scratch the two birthmarks on my right arm, then lift up my T-shirt to scratch the scars on my stomach. The stomach scars seem to burn today.

Mum's room is dark and the air is dank. She's been smoking in bed again. I like to keep my room dark too, but this is like a cave. She used to be an open-the-curtains-and-let-the-sunshine-in kind of person. Now she's hiding like some reclusive old movie star I saw in an old black-and-white film once.

I turn on the light to find her sitting on the end of the king size bed, her fingers clawing into the pale pink doona. She has her fancy silk dressing gown on but she seems lost in it. She is quite short, and super thin, with pale skin and short brown hair that is going grey. The dark circles under her eyes make her look way older than 42. Smoking like a chimney doesn't help.

I hate it that she gets thinner as I get fatter. I hate that I even have that thought.

'I barely slept last night. It was so hot with the broken air con. I'll have to call someone to come and fix it today.'

The white air conditioner unit hanging over her bed looks like a big toaster. At least she has one in her room. All I have is a ceiling fan that sounds like a creaking gate when it's switched on. It's the kind of thing Dad would try to fix, then stuff up, before Mum would have to call a technician in. He was terrible at fixing things, but loved any excuse to go to Bunnings to buy some new tool or gadget to try.

She stretches out her left leg, and I kneel down in front of her, grabbing one of her thick sand-coloured compression stockings. They are coiled on the bedroom floor from last night, like shucked snakeskins. She has to wear them to stop blood clots forming in her legs.

It's been nearly five years since the car accident, which was the worst thing ever, even counting the pandemic. Her pelvis was shattered in the crash and her legs were crushed. Despite all the rehab she's gone through over the years, she still has trouble walking properly, and her twisted legs are covered in ravines of broken, discoloured skin, the bulging veins colliding. Not nice to look at every day. So I get on with the job and we talk as if it is not happening. I slip her foot into the stocking and start to roll it up, slowly and carefully. She lets out a quiet cry of pain, but it's not as bad as some days.

'I need you to pick up my meds from the chemist. There's a prescription on the kitchen table.'

She tenses as I pull the stocking a bit harder to get it up and over her knee. From there she manages the rest on her own.

She takes a deep breath once the first stocking is done. I grab the second one and start the whole process again. I'm almost done when she says, 'Also, can you *please* mow the lawn on Saturday?'

'I said I would, didn't I?'

I pull up the second stocking over her knee sharply. She winces, and I feel guilty, but then she winks at me.

'Yes, you say you'll do things, but they don't always get done, do they Gussy?'

I roll my eyes and stand up. 'I'm not a kid.'

My T-shirt has ridden up over my flabby gut. Shit. I quickly pull it back down. Did she see the new cut? I look back to see her reaction, but her mind is clearly on other things. She's stretching out her legs, rotating her ankles in circles. Round and round and back again. Totally like my life lately. Ever since Dad died, she's treated me like I'm ten again, like we've gone back in time.

\* \* \*

In the kitchen I eat a big bowl of Coco Pops and watch the morning light shining through the window onto the central stainless steel island bench. My shadowy reflection is all stretched and thin on the tabletop. If only.

The island, like every surface in the house, is spotless and sparkling. You could do brain surgery in here. Mum hates mess of any kind. Maybe that's why she finds my hair annoying.

I flick through socials as I shovel the last of the Coco Pops into my mouth. I know I should eat a healthy breakfast blah blah blah, but I'd sooner be super fat than forced to eat muesli, which is basically just rope in a bowl.

Grabbing my backpack, I head out the back door, calling a goodbye to Mum as I go. I get my mountain bike from the backyard, and wheel it down our empty driveway at the side of the house, past the shed and my old cubbyhouse. Out on the footpath I turn around and look back at the house. The white weatherboards, the empty driveway, the lawn that really does need mowing. It's the only home I remember, but it hasn't felt like home since Dad died. It's like the fun and the good vibes went with him, leaving Mum and me and the house all wrong somehow. Lately I feel like I never belonged here in the first place.

The house is one of thirty in our street, directly over the road from the Hazleton railway line. Opposite our place there's this long, thin patch of grass which is generously called a park. It butts onto the railway line itself, which is raised high above street level, with grassy slopes leading down each side, covered in tall peppercorn trees. The park has a bench and a swing set. Two big stormwater tunnels run under the railway line, which people use to cross from one side of Hazleton to another.

I like living near the railway line, hearing the sound of trains whooshing past and the bells clanging at the level crossing further down the road. Reassuring somehow. It's like whatever happens, over the road the trains will still be running. A way home or an escape route.

It only takes ten minutes of slow bike riding to get to Hazleton High, but I still arrive a bit sweaty. The school is a bland white modern building with a flat roof, and a huge school crest over the front doors. The crest is of an emu and an owl standing together, under some words in Latin that apparently mean 'Strive for Know-ledge'. So cringe.

I meet up with my best friend Shell at the school gates, like I do most mornings. We're both in year nine and smart. Shell is tall and fat like me, with a really pretty face. She has large Emma Stone eyes and she wears tons of black eyeliner that make her death stares epic, all with this spiky crown of jet-black hair. She looks strong too, like she could beat you up with one hand while she texted with the other. Her arms are as big as mine, and we both think she should get them tatted one day.

She even has a psych like me, so we sometimes compare notes. Not the super personal stuff, we just bitch about them in general. Hers doesn't say anything except *And how does that make you feel?*, whereas mine always says *Let's unpack that* like, ten times a session. My feelings are not a suitcase.

When I first met Shell I was impressed by her attitude right away. I was a bit scared of her too, to be honest. She plonked herself down next to me in one class in the first week of year seven and stared me up and down before asking, 'Who do you crush on most in this room?' Before I even had a chance to respond, she pointed to Tim Maloney in the front row. He had yellowy-blonde hair and really big feet.

'Him?'

'How did you know that I like . . .'

Eye-roll from Shell. 'Oh, please.'

We've been friends ever since.

We like the same books, the same crime TV shows, the same podcasts. Basically anything with a big mystery arc that we can try and solve before the reveal, and then sit about feeling all smug about it when we do.

We think sport is for 'other' people. We also both hate airheads. Hazleton High is full of them. Like Mikey Collins, who said that he thought 'faecal' was a kind of mouse. Or Tiff Marginisky, whose hair extensions caught fire when she leaned too close to her 'enlightenment' candle. We're the fat kids sticking together, judging everyone else . . . very TV.

The other impressive thing about Shell is her interest in sustainability issues. She's already started a petition for the school canteen to only use local, ethically sourced food. And she's only using eco-eyeliner, whatever that is. I think it's both her passion but also a rebellion against her dad. She doesn't like that he does advisory work for companies with really bad environmental credentials.

Anyway, today we have English together first up. I used to like English, but this year we have sketchy Mr Greaseyhead as our teacher. He kinda redefines the word creepy. He has a thin little moustache and this weird soft voice that grates after a while. And the greasiest hair ever. You could fry chips in it, I reckon. He wears shirts that are a bit too tight and a pencil behind his ear. Who does that?

We sit next to one another in the back row and brace ourselves for another class about *Romeo and Juliet*.

My phone vibrates in my pocket. We're not allowed to have them in class, but we smuggle them in to stay sane. It's Shell of course.

*Juliet is so basic*

I glance her way. She's staring at Greaseyhead like he's an enemy agent.

*Do you wanna be Romeo?*

*Why do I need to be either?*

*[eyeroll emoji] You don't.*

*Want to hang after school?*

*I can't tonight – I have to do some shit for Mum and Kane.*

She stops texting and turns to me, when Greaseyhead is writing on the white board, and whispers: 'Your mother runs your life.'

'Yeah, I know.'

'And why are you spending so much time with Kane? Do you fancy him or something?'

'No, sicko, he's my oldest friend! He's giving me driving lessons.'

She tries to give me a death stare so I deflect it by pulling my sunnies down over my eyes, but Greasyhead spots me.

'Take those things off, Mr Green,' he snaps. 'You're not a rock star.'

Shell laughs like this was her plan all along. Her laugh is infectious, but Greasyhead is staring, so I have to cover my own smile with my hand.

Later we find our corner of the yard and sit with our lunch under an old gum tree to escape the sun. Hazleton High isn't so bad as schools go. It's not like those schools on TV where the kids are all hot, talk like self-aware grown-ups, and never seem to do homework. And there aren't the big class divisions that define lots of shows like that. Obviously we have the footy boys and the hot girls who chase the footy boys, but we also have theatre boys and music boys and indie boys, as well as footy girls and arty girls and chess girls. Still, Shell and I are the fattest kids in the school and we kinda own that.

'Did you listen to that podcast I sent you?' asks Shell, squishing some potato chips into her salad roll. It makes a satisfying crunch.

I shake my head, my mouth full of meat pie. 'Are those chips organic?'

She glares at me.

I laugh. 'You have even creepier taste in podcasts than me. I haven't listened to it yet. I've been caught up in cold case websites. I found some awesome ones the other day, old Australian crimes for once.'

Shell wags a finger at me dramatically. 'If you want to be a detective, you need to understand the criminal mind and how these people were caught. It's all about the psychology of crime, not just the forensics.'

'Thanks Enola Holmes,' I snicker.

She's right of course – she usually is. In school, in life. In who is into who at school.

She seems distracted today, staring into space.

'You okay?' I ask.

'Yes, fine,' she says, too quickly. 'Try and listen to the podcast tonight, it's really good.'

I'm not convinced by her change of subject. 'C'mon, what's up? Tell me.'

She crosses her legs back and forth and fiddles with the black leather band around her left wrist. I feel like she's going to change the subject again, but she finally speaks.

'It's super weird, but I have this feeling like my brain is out of sync with my body.'

'What do you mean?'

She sighs. 'Like who I am on the inside is not who I'm meant to be on the outside.'

'Like how?' I laugh awkwardly.

She shakes her head, clearly frustrated. 'It's like an emotional and a physical thing. Like something . . . it's hard to explain.'

The end of lunch siren blares. 'Let's talk more another time.' She scrambles to her feet, grabs her bag, and walks off without looking back.

* * *

After school, I go to pick up Mum's medicine, like I'm her servant or something. She may not be able to drive anymore, but she could still get a cab. She has this special discount card that she hardly ever uses – too proud – which is nuts. I tried to get her to download the Uber app but she wasn't interested.

Standing at the pharmacy counter, I feel like I'm her carer, not her son. Still, at least the air con is blasting in here. Outside, the heat slaps me and I'm drenched in sweat by the time I get to Kane's place. My school uniform is sticking to my stomach, so I have to pluck my shirt free once I get off my bike. *Argh.*

Kane Parker and I have lived next door to each other forever. Kane's three years older than me, he's got his driver's licence, he's blond, good-looking, popular, works out a *lot* and is good at sport (especially footy). He's basically everything I will never be, even if I wanted to.

We're so different. On paper we probably shouldn't be friends. On TV he'd totally be my bully. But, like me, he doesn't have any brothers or sisters, so he has become like a big brother to me over the years. And he's a big *Doctor Who* fan like me, even though he likes the Daleks while I much prefer the Cybermen. Underneath the blokey exterior and the gym routine, he's a bit of a nerd.

Our mums kinda pushed us together when we moved here, likely hoping my studious brain would rub off on him, and his exercise obsession would rub off on me. A total fail on both fronts. It was probably also so that they could have their wine sessions in the garden in peace, and not need to watch us all the time. So, while we didn't change one another, we did become friends. We both know that we're clichés, but that's half the fun.

Plus I totally saved his life once . . .

One of the things I really like about him is that he's a black-and-white kind of guy, whereas I feel like I'm every shade of grey. He's a car that speeds full throttle to where it needs to get to, while my wheels are turning in different directions, going nowhere.

As I walk down his driveway, I spot him out the back by the granny flat. His Granny literally used to live there until she passed away. The flat is just two rooms: the main room, with a double bed (never made), an old sofa that had once been in his parents' lounge, his family's abandoned TV (with an Xbox, obviously), and a kitchenette with a bar fridge (always full of beer). The second room is just a tiny bathroom.

I hang out here a lot after school. He's here all the time, 'cos he's done with high school and he's not playing footy anymore since he stuffed up his right knee last year. Plus he has Netflix and Stan and Foxtel and Disney and Prime, as well as a couple of sports channels I've never even heard of.

Kane is bent over, blacking the tyres of his new-but-really-old 1970s Kingswood. Four-litre engine. Vinyl bench seats. Three-on-the-tree gears. It's baby-shit brown, which is hilarious. He saved up for ages for this car, and plans to restore it properly. Blacking its tyres is it a bit much though, like rolling a turd in glitter.

He gives me a blokey wave as he sees me. 'Hey Goose.' (He misheard my name when we first met as little kids and it stuck.)

'Nice crack,' I say as I walk over to him. He rolls his eyes and pulls up his pants. 'You know this is an old petrol guzzler. Totally bad for the environment.'

He snorts. 'Do you want another driving lesson or not?'

'Yes. Mum still hasn't booked me any.'

Kane has been giving me lessons on the sly. There are only a few weeks till I'm sixteen and I'm super keen to get my Learner's so I can start driving lessons properly. Not that Mum will go with me.

Even though Dad's Volkswagen Jetta was written off in the accident, we still have Mum's old Ford Focus. It's just sitting there in the shed untouched. I know that she worries that I'll get my licence and then go and have some horror car accident, just like the one that killed Dad and injured her. I get it – it's triggering for her. But I need my licence to get into the police one day, and to have a life beyond compression stockings and pharmacy runs.

In the driver's seat, the vinyl seat that's been soaking up the sun all day warms my arse. He slides into the passenger side carefully, hand on his right knee. 'Righto, let's do this,' he says.

Kane stuffed his knee playing footy. He went up for a big hero-type of mark, and got it, but landed real bad. He said he heard his knee make this brutal sound and he knew it was gone. He did in his ACL – whatever that means.

The steering wheel is super hot too, despite the ugly orange towelling-cover-thing he's got on it. His car has an awkward old three-gear stick shift that you have to really pull in hard to shift gears. I start the engine and bunny-hop up his driveway. I always do this, but only because the clutch is so stiff. I turn left into our street and drive a few blocks to a nearby car park to practise parking.

'You're getting better,' he says as I zoom around the roundabout and slide smoothly into the car park. The car is big and old and hard to manoeuvre, and it feels like I'm driving a tank.

It's the reverse parks that do me in. I botch the first attempt. He laughs. 'Well, that sucked. Try again.'

Second one is the same. And the third.

I bang my hands against the steering wheel as I fail the fourth time.

'Next time, Goose,' he smiles.

\* \* \*

Back at Kane's place, we sit down to watch *Doctor Who* before I head home. Kane lowers himself onto the sofa gingerly, keeping his right knee soft, not straightening it out completely, making sure it's supported.

For the hundredth time I stare at his official, signed, limited edition *Doctor Who* posters framed on the walls, one for each Doctor. His pride and joy. I swear their eyes follow me around the room.

While he's deciding which episode to watch, I start browsing through this awesome unsolved crime website I found a couple of nights ago. It focuses on missing kids. I've been pretty obsessed with true crime ever since I was old enough to watch cop shows and movies. I've always liked stories about missing people, about what happens to them, and what happens to the families and friends left behind. Once I found this site, I plummeted down a crime rabbit hole in the middle of the night. I love that it has Australian cases on it, not just American or UK ones like most other sites.

Kane leans back on the sofa. 'Let's watch a Flux episode. How long have you got before you have to get home?'

'Not too long. Lately Mum's been wanting me to stay home all the time. It's like she's keeping me close, treating me like a kid.'

'She's okay, your mum.'

'What, 'cos you both go to the same physio, suddenly you're mates?'

Kane laughs. 'Hardly. But it's hard when parts of your body hurt and you can't do what you used to do. Like, I miss not being able to play footy big time, but it's worse when even just walking hurts. My knee is getting better, but it's taking too long. It's really shitting me.'

'Oh, right. That sounds depressing.'

'No, just frustrating. I can't do much exercise, just arm weights now.

Driving's okay, but I need to stretch a lot. Makes me feel super unfit.'

He's amazing. It's still heaps more than I do. But I get it, fitness is his thing and it's been taken away.

'Still, your arms will be huge by the end of summer, all that extra time spent on them.'

He smirks at me and flexes. 'A hundred percent. Sun's out, guns out.'

'You're such a cliché Kane.'

'Says the guy with the rainbow wristband,' he snickers.

I totally forgot I had that on today.

'I'm more than footy and muscles you know, just like you're more than a rainbow bracelet.'

'What else are you then?' I laugh.

Kane's face is serious. I feel like I've struck a nerve, but he changes the subject. 'What're you looking at that's so interesting, anyway?'

'I've found this site about missing kids. Can't stop looking at it. There are loads of kids, page after page.'

'Weirdo.'

'Himbo,' I reply, then show him my phone. 'They use this AI to "age" old photos. So, if you were taken like twenty years ago they can guess what you'd look like now, years later.'

'It's so strange that you like this stuff,' he says. Still, he has a closer look.

I start flicking through the site for him. On the left-hand side of the screen are pictures of missing kids from when they disappeared. On the right-hand side it shows what some AI estimates that they would look like five, ten, twenty years later.

There is something about the expressions on the aged-up faces that spooks me. Like they are trying to reach out to me from the screen. I shiver.

Kane takes my phone and starts to browse through the pages

himself. 'Shit, these AI photos are spooky, aren't they?' he says, as he keeps flicking through, face after face.

'Wait!' I yell. *It can't be . . .*

'What?'

'Go back a page, quick!'

'What's wrong?'

'Just do it!' My heart's racing like crazy. I feel like I'm going to have a panic attack. Shit.

Kane flicks back to the previous page.

'There, that kid.' I grab my phone and point. 'Look at his square head . . . he looks just like me. That kid *is* me!'

# Chapter 2

# Website

I am staring at a photo of me. Well, not exactly, but close enough that I don't know what to think. A missing kid that looks like me. What?

The kid's name is Robin Winter. He *really* looks like me. I touch my face as if I need to check that it hasn't suddenly disappeared and reappeared in the photo. In the original picture of Robin as a toddler, he looks cute, happy, staring right at the camera. The site says he was three years old when he was taken in 2010.

There are no pictures, physical or digital, of me when I was this young. It always seemed weird that there weren't any, and Mum and Dad were super evasive if I ever asked about it.

The 'now' photo looks so much like me it gives me the creeps. It's a strange photo. When you look really closely you can tell that it's a fake. There's a stretchiness to some parts of it, a smoothing the AI does based on the original photo. But it *still* looks like me.

It says Robin was born on 20 November 2007, the same year as me but a month earlier, and snatched from his home in Bellanta on the afternoon of 1 March 2010 while his mother was asleep.

In my head there's this rush of feelings, all jumbled up like the junk drawer in our kitchen. It obviously can't be real. It's just a nutty coincidence. Life is full of them, right?

Kane takes my phone back and has a closer look. 'Let's chuck it up on the screen.' He fiddles around until the website comes up on his big screen TV. His eyes widen a bit, then he laughs awkwardly.

'Same boof head. Were you kidnapped and your parents forgot to tell you?'

I know he's joking but I do wonder. 'Well, he's the right age . . .'

'Still, it obviously isn't you.'

I can't take my eyes off the screen.

'Obviously.' I try to slow my breathing, like my psych taught me.

'Dude, are you a spy? Is Angus Green an alias?'

'Ha, totally. Maybe I'm in some kind of witness protection program?'

'Or are you this kid's long-lost twin?'

'What if I was cloned? There could be more of me floating around.'

'Mate, more than one of you is too freaky to think about.'

'Like another one of you would be any better.'

Kane snorts. 'I have to admit, it does look like you. But they say everyone has a double somewhere, don't they?'

I take the phone back and shake my head. It can't be me.

We both lean in for a closer look at the TV. 'What else does it say?' asks Kane.

'Just some stuff about the case. There's a contact button for any info.'

That face. Robin's face. It's like looking in a mirror, but then not at the same time. Like a distorted circus mirror, or a bad photo taken on a weird angle.

Kane reaches over to his bar fridge and grabs a couple of beers. He cracks a can for himself and one for me. I take a swig. Beer always tastes too bitter to me but the buzz is worth it.

He cheers. 'Here's to Robin Winter, the lost boy.' We clink our cans together.

I chug half my can. Too quick.

'Will you ask your mum about this, Goose?'

'As if! She'd go crazy.'

'True. Probably not a good idea.'

Yeah, asking Mum if I have a missing twin or if I was kidnapped is a dangerous move.

'Well, you say you wanna be a cop, then act like a cop. In-vest-i-gate!' he snickers.

He's right, I should be finding out more. Taking control.

Kane disconnects my phone and we watch TV for a while, but my mind is on that website. Soon I have to go, so I rummage around in my bag for chewy to cover my beer breath. I say goodbye to him as he's gingerly stretching out his leg. Guess he's been sitting in the one position too long.

That photo of Robin Winter is sticking in my head. I know it's impossible, yet I feel queasy. Probably just the beer, but still . . . what are the chances of having a double?

For some reason, instead of going home I go right past my house and walk my bike along the edge of the park. I lean my bike against a bench and squeeze myself into one of the swings. I have another good look at the photo, slowly swinging back and forth.

*What if this Robin kid is my missing twin?* I laugh out loud. I'm being paranoid. This is all just a freaky coincidence.

# Chapter 3

# Wine

I slide my bike in the rack in the driveway at home and go to turn the corner into the backyard but stop when I hear Mum and Fiona, Kane's mum, talking under the verandah. They are in their traditional wine-drinking positions: laying back on our banana lounges, ice bucket with a bottle of white wine between them, glasses clinking, gossip flowing.

I lean against the wall of the house and listen to their conversation. Surveillance practice. Cops have to be good at surveillance. I grab my phone, open the camera and tilt it round the corner, just enough so I can see them.

Fiona is lean and blonde, and full of energy, like her son. She always has a tight ponytail that bobs up and down as she speaks, which is fast and often. She's in sports gear as usual, like she's about to go for a run or just back from one. Proper sports gear too, and crazy expensive running shoes. Kane's dad Brian is like a male version of her, minus the ponytail. I swear no one in that family owns real shoes, just runners.

Fiona is looking down at Mum's legs. 'Those look red today, hon.'

'This heat makes them crazy itchy,' Mum replies, somehow laughing and sighing at the same time. Her voice sounds far away.

'The weather is punishing. I could barely get through my run this morning. But I did, so I've earned my wine.' Not for the first time I wonder if Fiona does all this exercise just so she can drink more.

I can just see Mum as she drops some ice cubes into her glass, before lifting it to her forehead, rolling it back and forth.

'You look tired Meg,' Fiona says, knocking back her wine like it's a protein shake.

'Thanks!' Mum laughs. 'Yeah, I am tired. The bloody air con's died so it was hot as hell last night. There's a guy coming round to fix it later, thank God.'

'Must be rough.' Fiona says in a sympathetic voice.

Mum sighs. 'I'm in constant pain, I can't walk very far, I can't drive, I can't work. And the heat just exacerbates everything.'

'I can only imagine,' Fiona says, looking down at her own toned, tanned legs.

Mum smiles at her. 'Sorry, the heat is making me crabby. I do look tired. Always have. Right up 'til she died, my mother used to tell me to smile all the time. She said I always looked disappointed. I hear those words every morning when I look in the mirror.'

'That was shitty of her!'

Mum shrugs sadly. 'Still, Tom always used to make me smile.'

'I know it's tough with him gone.'

Mum nods. 'Yes, I miss my old partner in crime. Anyway, enough sad talk. What's Kane up to? Gus tells me nothing, he's so secretive these days.'

*Am I?*

Fiona shakes her head, frowning. 'He had no luck getting an apprenticeship anywhere, which is a shame. He was already struggling at school when the pandemic hit, so I understand why he wanted to get out of there, but I told him over and over not to leave without a job or apprenticeship lined up. Would he listen to me? No. Plus, he's hated missing footy this season because of his knee. Thank God he's got McDonald's part-time. I only let him take three-hour shifts so it's not too much pressure on his knee. I'd rather he didn't work at all while he's recovering, but he was getting so down.'

'Really? He seems fine at physio,' Mum says.

'Trust me, he needs to keep busy. And doing weights and working on that old car aren't enough. Mind you, seeing you have the same physio, you probably know more about his recovery than I do. He never tells me anything unless I nag it out of him.'

Mum nods. 'Paul has said that he's rushing it, trying to recover too fast. But that's all he'll tell me.'

'That sounds about right. On that note, how's Gus going with his new therapist?'

'Okay, I think. He shows up at least. Dr Yamada confirms that with me each week. But I don't really know if it's having much of an impact. I don't think he's hurting himself anymore, but I can't be sure. And if I ask him all hell breaks loose, so I just watch him like a hawk, looking for signs, good or bad.'

*I can't believe she's telling Fiona this!* But it would explain why she's always up in my face.

Fiona goes to say something and somehow spills some of her wine over her overly branded top. 'Ah, crap.'

I can't stop myself from laughing a little. Mum hears me.

'Snooping are we, Gussy?' she calls out in her 'you're in trouble' voice, this weirdly controlled yell. She turns back to Fiona. 'He likes to think he's a boy detective. It *used* to be cute.'

I come around the corner with my backpack in front of me like a shield.

'No, I was just . . . um . . . I dropped my wallet.'

'Sure you did,' she laughs.

'Hi Gus,' Fiona says, patting away at her shirt.

Mum gives me one of her looks that tells me she's going to explain something simple to me in a really patronising way.

'Now, the air con man will be here in thirty minutes, so make yourself useful and help him so he can get the job done quickly. He'll charge like a wounded bull otherwise.'

'I should go home and change this top,' says Fiona. She finishes her drink and stands up. 'Give me a call if the tradie's hot, hon!' she calls, and disappears with a fluttering wave.

Mum smiles as she goes. 'Will do.'

Mum holds out her hand to me as if she is royalty. I take it and help her out of her chair. She struggles to stand at first, but once she is up she's okay. We head into the lounge room, still stuffy from last night's heat. Mum looks around, probably checking that everything is neat and tidy as usual, then turns to me. With my sweaty shirt, I'm not tidy at all. I probably don't pass muster. Avoiding her eyes, I head to the kitchen and put the meds I picked up for her in the pantry as usual.

Mum's phone pings. She sighs as she reads a text. 'Damn, the air con guy has cancelled.'

'Want me to have a go first?' I ask. It's not like I actually know what to do, but it's the kind of thing Dad would do.

She shrugs and follows me to her room. I grab the air con remote from her bedside table and turn it on. A terrible clanging sound comes out as its long slit of a mouth opens up. Plenty of noise but no air.

Sighing, she takes the remote off me and sits it next to the instruction manual and the warranty document she has somehow found, lined up side-by-side with military precision.

I need to prove I don't need to be babied. With the manual in one hand, I stand on the bed and pull the outer front section of the unit off. It just looks like the air filter is blocked.

'This is full of gunk,' I say, showing Mum. I carefully pull it out of the unit and take it outside into the yard to wash it under the tap. When it's clean and dry, I put it back in and turn the unit on. Just like that, cool air is blowing out, almost silently. I can't believe it worked. I'm feeling quite smug now.

Mum actually claps her hands. 'Well done you,' she says.

'See, I'm not a kid anymore,' I mutter.

She looks at me strangely. 'I never said you were.'

Five minutes later, she's lying back on the bed, enjoying the cold air on her face and legs. I'm itchy and rubbing the cuts on my stomach through my shirt.

'Did you hurt yourself?' she asks in a worried voice. I remember what she said about watching me like a hawk.

'No, just itchy,' I mumble. 'I'll wash up outside so I don't dirty up the bathroom.'

She reaches out to me. 'You'd tell me if you were hurting yourself again, wouldn't you?' She draws me close to her. 'When's your next appointment with Dr Yamada?'

I pull away gently. 'Next Wednesday.'

'And you think he's helping?'

I do. 'Yes. Him and the meds.'

'Good,' she says as she rubs her legs again. She's probably in pain. Not the time to bring up wild missing twin theories. But soon.

# Chapter 4

# Socials

Later that night, alone in my room, I'm sitting in bed thinking about that photo again. On my laptop, I take another look at the website, concentrating on the wording, trying to pull it apart like a puzzle. Next to the photos of Robin, there's a scan of an article from the *Bellanta Courier*.

*SEEKING ROBIN WINTER*

*On 1 March 2010, Bellanta Police received a call from Ms Jane Winter, who reported her two-year-old son Robin missing. He had been playing in the front yard of the Winter home when Ms Winter had taken a nap at 3 pm. When she woke up at 5 pm he was nowhere to be seen.*

*A comprehensive search took place with police and locals sweeping the town and surrounding areas. Divers searched the local creek. Hospitals in the region were contacted. Unfortunately, Robin seemed to have disappeared without a trace.*

*The investigation was led by Detective Frank Firelli of the Bellanta police. Initially, police suspected Mark Reynolds, a former boyfriend of Ms Winter, was involved, but he had a strong alibi and was never charged. Three other people were interviewed in connection to the crime, none of whom were charged. Ms Winter's family were cleared of any involvement and Robin's father is unknown.*

*Specialist police from Sydney were engaged to aid in the investigation, but despite all efforts, Robin has never been found.*

**This is a computer-generated image of what Robin could look like now, aged roughly fifteen. If you have seen Robin or have any information about him, click the contact button below.**

I shut my laptop and roll over to try to go to sleep, but I'm still awake at 3 am. Wide awake. Staring at the ceiling, I trace the outline of the old ceiling rose pattern in my mind. After a while I give up, and focus instead on how hot it still is, and the creaking of the ceiling fan. Anything to turn my mind off. It doesn't work. I pick up my phone and stare at the photo again. The entry was last updated six months ago, which means Robin is still missing all these years later.

I end up spending the rest of the night with my brain spinning into overdrive, thinking about the website and Robin and Jane and Mum and Dad.

It can't be me. But what if it is? What if Mum isn't my real mum or Dad wasn't my real dad? We sure don't look like one another. But if it were true, what does that make Mum and Dad – my kidnappers?
*Shit.*

My feelings roll around my stomach like fishhooks, digging into me from the inside. I realise I've always felt out of sync with the world. Slower, clumsier, sluggishly dragging myself through life like the air is made of tar. It's not just about being fat; it's like every part of me is wrong. The world seems to operate on a different speed to me, and I'm always struggling just to keep up.

Could I be Robin? Is that why I feel this way?

I'm never going to get to sleep, so I move to my desk, pulling up the website entry for Robin on my laptop again.

I keep staring at the contact button underneath. Who is on the other side of that? Should I just ask? I take a deep breath and click. An email window opens up.

I'm not really sure what to say, but I start typing anyway

*Hi, I may have some information about Robin . . .*

Wait. What am I even doing? This is nuts. I don't have information, just a weird feeling.

But I send it anyway.

I wait. Nothing happens. I snort at myself for thinking there would be an instant reply or something.

Suddenly it hits me. A kidnapping would generate lots of media attention, so there should be heaps of articles about the case. Plus, if my kid was taken, I would splash my story all over socials so they could find me if they wanted to. If Robin's case was online, surely it would have been a relative that posted it. Someone approved the use of the photos and the information. Someone signed up for the service. Someone out there wants to find Robin.

I start with the *Bellanta Courier* website, but it wasn't properly online back then, so there's not much I can get from their digital archives that isn't covered in the scanned article. Searching wider, I find quite a few pieces on the original case, but they all have the same information about the case, Robin, and Jane, and the occasional mention that Mark Reynolds was a suspect but was never charged. Others mention that Jane's family were cleared and that Robin's father was unknown. Does that just mean they didn't know who he was, or that even Jane didn't know?

The articles all have the same picture of Robin, looking small and innocent, staring at the camera with a toy dinosaur in his hand. I can't connect to the picture at all. There's a picture of Jane in some of the articles, which must have been taken before Robin went missing. She is a pretty blonde with sparkly eyes. Later articles have a picture of her doing media with the police. She looks thin, haggard and worn out, her dark roots showing.

I look up Jane Winter on Facebook. I get about eighty results. None of the profiles seem to match the pictures I have of Jane, and none of them mention Bellanta, though she could have moved. If your kid was kidnapped, would you stay where he was taken from in case he escaped and came back? Or would you leave and start a new life?

I look up Robin Winter next. There are two hundred or so variations of that name online, and none of them look like him, or me. Some are girls. I'm not really sure if Facebook allows photos of missing people anyway, with all their complex rules.

There aren't any results for Detective Frank Firelli. But I've read that cops are rarely on socials.

I collapse back on my bed, suddenly exhausted. I start scrolling through the family photos I have stored on my phone. Mum, Dad, me. Heaps of memories, but I haven't had a phone long enough for me to have any from years ago, except a few Mum shared of her and Dad's wedding day and of her when she was younger. I have none from when I was younger. I can't stop my brain now. What if every one of these photos is part of one big lie? What if I'm the biggest lie of all? I'd know if I was kidnapped, I'd remember . . . something. No, Kane's right. It's just a weird coincidence.

I need to speak to Dr Yamada. Even better, I need to speak to Shell. Fishhooks again.

## Chapter 5

# Charger

School sucks today. I'm exhausted and my head is pounding. I feel like I have some kind of emotional hangover.

I need to see Shell. She always knows what to do. She'll tell me I shouldn't even waste two brain cells thinking about this, and then I can forget it and get on with the rest of my boring life.

I'm not in a class with her until later, so I spend the morning refreshing my email to see if there's a reply from the website.

I finally catch up with Shell outside the media room.

'Did you listen to that pod I sent you?' she asks. She's wearing less eyeliner than usual. Maybe one of the teachers has told her off.

'I need to talk to you about something weird that happened yesterday,' I blurt.

'Gossip!' Shell virtually pushes me through the door of the classroom. We sit down at some desks at the back, underneath various movie posters pinned to the wall.

I tell her everything, showing her the photo and the website.

'This *literally* could be you,' she says, lapping up the drama.

'I know, right? I mean, it can't be me, obviously.'

'No, totally, it can't be.' She doesn't quite meet my eyes.

Still, I feel better now. I put my phone away and we talk about other stuff for a while, including another podcast she is obsessed with (something about what psycho killers eat for breakfast), and whether or not Janey Simonson is pregnant ('I swear I heard it kicking in Maths'), and how the planet is heating up. But every now and then she looks my way with an odd expression.

'What is it?' I ask, when I notice the weird look a third time.

She shrugs. 'What if there *is* more to this photo?' She fiddles with her black leather bracelet.

'I thought we agreed there couldn't be?'

She grabs my hand. 'Look. You often tell me you feel way out of place in your family, right? And you don't look like either of your parents. Maybe there's a reason for that, is all I'm saying.'

She's trying to shit-stir me, which she does really well, but I'm not buying it.

'Could be heaps of reasons for that. It doesn't mean anything.'

She lets my hand go. 'Of course. It's just a joke.' She pauses. 'Will you show your mum this photo?'

'No. It'd upset her. Or make her angry. Both, actually.'

'I guess it's a pretty random thing to bring up out of nowhere.' She's silent for a moment. 'But it's not like there's ever gonna be a logical time to bring up kidnapping either. It'll be super weird, any time you ask.'

'I can't do it. Firstly, it's not even a thing. And secondly, how do I even ask? Like, "Hey, did you kidnap me years ago but forget to mention it?" No way!'

Shell's eyes widen as she laughs. 'No, not like that. But I guess if you ask her in a serious way, then that implies that you think it could be real.'

'Exactly.'

We stare at each other. She raises her eyebrow, not blinking, but I hold her gaze. It's a dare, but we both know I can't do it.

Her phone pings, breaking the spell. She looks at the text and rolls her eyes. 'Cheryl's off on one. She's such a drama queen! She wants me to grow my hair out and stop dyeing it black, and basically look pretty like *she* was in high school. They didn't have Instagram bitches making everyone feel worthless back then.'

I snort. 'Yup.'

She picks at her black nail polish. 'Y'know, I'm an embarrassment to her. Cheryl had one of her posh skinny friends over the other day and she gave me such side-eye. Cheryl's big too but she hides it like it's some guilty secret. Then when I stumble through the door like a big mess I shame her in front of her friends.'

'No way is your mum ashamed of you.'

'She is. And Larry's no better, with his rich business bros judging me when they visit . . . I don't mind being fat, but I don't like the way they look at me.'

Shell often speaks like this. She hates that her dad makes a ton of money advising big fossil fuel emitting companies. Her family have a holiday house that they rarely use, and they go overseas twice a year.

She rubs her hand through her hair. 'I need to talk to them about how I'm feeling, but I can't right now. I'd just disappoint them.'

'What are you feeling?'

'Y'know. Gender stuff. The more Cheryl pushes for me to be girly, the weirder things are becoming for me.'

'So you think you're non-binary?' I had been wondering if this was what was going on with her, but it felt wrong to push her. It's her story to tell.

'No, it's not that simple. You don't just question something and then slap a label on it. It's complex.' She frowns, clearly frustrated with me.

'Okay, sorry. Want to talk about it?'

'It's a conversation I'm having with myself. Like, where do I fit in within myself? I don't feel like I present as "me" sometimes.' She shakes her head. Things are quietly tense with us for a moment. Suddenly she burps and we both laugh.

'Anyway, that's enough me talk. What are you going to do now?'

'Dunno. I've emailed the contact on the website. I've stalked my way through socials but I can't find Robin or Jane.'

'Maybe just see if anything comes of the email before you do anything else. And try not to overthink it.'

I nod. She's right. Decisions seem to come easy to her. And Kane. Just not me.

'Yeah, Kane said the same thing.'

Her death stare burns like the sun.

'He was there when I found the photo,' I add quickly. Shell rolls her eyes.

I hear someone clear their throat and realise that while we have been talking, the classroom has filled up. People are staring. Awkward.

Mr Carlson, the goofy media teacher, raises his thick Muppet eyebrows and turns to the class.

'Okay people. This is the part where we all sit down and shut up. The bell has rung and it's time to focus.'

Shell gives him the double bird while his back is turned. It's her go-to move, and she wears it well.

There's so much to talk about that we ditch the rest of our classes for the day. We hang out in the empty lot on the other side of the railway tunnels, out of sight of my house. Shell takes a packet of smokes out of her backpack and lights one up. 'One of Cheryl's fancy friends left these behind.' She waves the pack at me, offering me one, but I shake my head. I hate them.

'Do you smoke to help you lose weight?'

'No, you know I don't care about being fat. I just like smoking. Your mum smokes like a train . . . does she do it to stay thin?' Shell blows a smoke ring in my direction. 'If she really *is* your mother.'

'Stop it.' I laugh.

'We should solve this case together. You know all the police procedural side and I know the psychology. We look at the world differently than other people. If we teamed up, we'd be unstoppable.'

Funny that whenever she talks like this I instantly believe her. Dunno if it's her charisma or if she hypnotises me with her confidence or something, but I agree. 'Let's do it then. Let's become unstoppable detectives.'

We spend the next hour or so wheeling out different scenarios of what it would mean if it turned out I was Robin after all.

Shell is full of ideas.

'You could get on *The Project.*'

'Maybe a Netflix series?' I add.

'You could get your own reality show. "Help, I Was Kidnapped, Get Me Out of Here!"' She sniggers. 'Or a big family reunion in Bellanta. Street parade. Meet the mayor.'

'I could write a book – *The Kidnap Games.*'

We're still laughing and spouting off stupid theories when I remember to check my phone. It's dead as.

'Shell, can I borrow your power bank? My phone's out of juice.'

She rummages around in her bag and brings out the charger.

I plug my phone in and within seconds it springs to life with six missed calls and a text from Mum in all caps.

*WHERE ARE YOU? I NEED YOUR HELP!*

'Shit, I have to go Shell. Sorry!'

'I hope everything's okay,' she calls out to me as I run back through the tunnel and over the road home. As I run, I listen to each voicemail with a sinking heart. Mum's voice sounds more desperate with every message, pleading for me to come home.

* * *

By the time I get home I feel sick. I run through the front door calling out to her, rushing around the house till I find her on the floor in her bedroom.

She is crumpled between the bed and the far window, rocking back and forth like an upturned turtle. She looks terrible. She is sweaty and her hair is plastered to her head. Her legs are red and swollen, as bad as I have ever seen them. Her veins are purple and bulging, looking as if they're going to burst.

'Mum. Did you take your meds? Where are your meds?'

She shudders, her dark puddled eyes opening wide at the sound of my voice.

'Where have you been?' she cries.

I kneel down and try to help her up but she just keeps rocking back and forth on the floor, staring at me.

'Just at school. My phone died.'

'I can't find my new prescription. You said you put it in the pantry but it's not there.'

'I did put it in there, same as always. I'll get it for you, hang on.'

I run to the pantry, searching the shelf where we keep her medication. The medicine isn't there, but I *know* I put it away yesterday.

My heart is pounding a million beats an hour, like I am running for my life. Where is it? I start pulling cans out of the pantry, pushing stuff around desperately. I drop down on my knees to search the bottom shelves, and finally I find it. The packet must have fallen down and rolled under the shelf somehow.

I grab the packet and stand up, relief flooding my body. On my way back to her room, I spot a nearly empty wine bottle on the kitchen bench. Did she drink that before she went looking for her meds and accidentally drop them down here? Or did she drink because she couldn't find the medicine?

Mum's eyes are open even wider, but at least she isn't crying now. I take her hand and help her up onto the bed, lifting her legs and resting them on two pillows while she takes her medicine. Her breathing slows down and her eyelids start to droop. I sit there holding her hand for about twenty minutes until she drifts off to sleep.

'I'm sorry,' I whisper to her as I put her hand down by her side and quietly leave the room.

In the kitchen I struggle for breath. I haven't seen her that bad for a long time. What if I had stayed out longer with Shell? What might have happened? Why didn't she call her doctor, or Fiona?

It's all my fault. I should have been keeping an eye on my phone. I should have been thinking about her, not out talking about this kidnap rubbish with Shell. I feel sick thinking about what she'll say about this tomorrow.

# Chapter 6

# Cubby

I wake up with a start, like I've fallen asleep in class. Remembering Mum's incident last night, I guiltily slide back under the doona and hide. Still, it's Saturday, so I don't have to deal with school. I can stay home and make sure she is okay. I have a shift at McDonald's at 4 pm, but I might call in sick if she's still bad by then.

I look in on her about 9.30 am but she's still out of it. Good sign. She has kicked off her sheets, exposing her very red legs. I gently pull up the sheets to hide them. Poor Mum.

I sat up half the night after she took her meds, convinced that something else was going to go wrong, or that they would wear off. But no sounds came from her room, apart from the odd snore.

Maybe this is punishment for getting caught up in this stupid kidnap theory? Maybe it's a sign to leave it alone?

It's been two nights in a row I've had hardly any sleep. I am wrecked.

Shell keeps texting to see if everything is fine. I don't want to get into it, so I tell her things are okay.

I stay in my room, trying not to disturb Mum. I play some childish online game, listen to music with my headphones, start reading a book, but I can't focus. I even try to do some homework! The heat isn't letting up. I want to go for a swim or just go somewhere cooler, but I'm afraid to leave her alone in the house.

I keep looking in on her every hour or so. She is still asleep at 1 pm. Same at 2 pm. And 3 pm. I call Maria, my shift manager, and croak out a story about a sore throat. Not sure if she believes me, but she tells me to get well soon anyway.

In the end I must have nodded off myself because I wake up around 5 pm. I jump up out of bed and immediately feel lightheaded. I rush over to Mum's room but she's not there, and the bed is made.

*Where is she?* I find her out the backyard doing some re-potting on the outdoor table, like it's any other day. She is resting on one of the bar stools from the kitchen and she has her bright pink gardening gloves on.

'How are you?' I ask tentatively.

She looks at me with this kinda blank, controlled face. 'Fine. You left me in a very bad position yesterday.'

'I'm so sorry Mum. The medicine had fallen under the bottom shelf.'

'If you'd picked up your phone, things wouldn't have gotten that bad. I'm very disappointed in you.'

I look down at my feet. Those quiet words are much harsher than any yelling. They're like a slap to the face. She's making me pay in her own way.

'Where were you anyway? I rang the school, and they said they couldn't find you.'

*Gulp.*

'Messing about with Shell?'

I nod.

She looks back at the plant she's potting, her mouth a bit pouty. 'She's a big influence on you isn't she?'

'So what if she is?'

She points her gardening trowel at me. 'That girl is not what she seems.'

'What does that even mean?'

'It's a feeling. She's hiding something.'

I can't believe she's throwing shade at Shell. Now I'm angry. The words come out before I can stop myself.

'Since you want to talk about hiding things, why do I have no relatives, no cousins, no grandparents? What happened to yours and Dad's parents?'

She turns away and rests her hands slowly and deliberately on the table. When she looks at me again, her voice is quieter than before, like she's tired.

'Tom grew up in a foster home, and I lost my parents when I was your age. You know this already. How many times—'

'Why are there no photos of me as a baby? Or a toddler?'

*Am I actually starting to believe I am Robin? Why can't I drop this?*

Her face red, she picks up the trowel again and goes back to her gardening. 'I've told you all of this before. Over and over. We lost all the photos when someone broke into the house years ago and took all our cameras and computer gear.'

'Wouldn't you have had some photos on your phone?'

She stares at me, eyebrows raised. 'No, I used to download photos onto my computer because phones didn't have much storage back then. Angus, what's going on?'

'I've got something you need to see.'

She fiddles with the plant she's working on. 'This Adenium has finally grown out of its pot. Look at that mess of roots,' she says, holding up the plant. The roots are tightly tangled around one another, trapped into a hard, unnatural mound like frozen worms.

'Have a look at this.' I hand her my phone.

She takes off her gloves and looks at the website. Her body seems to stiffen. 'What am I looking at?'

I zoom in on the photo and turn the phone back to her, watching her response closely.

She stares at me expressionlessly. 'And who is this?'

'Me,' I say impatiently, 'or at least it's a photo of someone who looks just like me. From a site about missing children.'

'It's not you,' she laughs lightly, but her smile doesn't reach her eyes.

'You don't think this kid looks just like me?'

'No. What are you suggesting?' She looks puzzled.

How do I say this when I'm still not sure if I believe this is me? 'I don't know. I just feel like I don't fit in anywhere.'

'There's nothing wrong with being a bit different. I thought you and Dr Yamada were starting to figure this out, trying to manage your anxiety?'

'Yes, but it's more than just anxiety . . .'

She comes up and puts her arms around me. 'If this is about yesterday, I'm not angry anymore. It's forgotten.'

She doesn't understand. But then again, neither do I.

'Maybe I have a double out there somewhere?'

She shakes her head. 'It's just a made-up image. You're talking as if this boy is real. I think this is just your anxiety expressing itself in a different way.'

'He's real enough to someone. They put his photo on a missing kid website.'

'Well, maybe—'

'Could I have a missing twin?'

'How could that have happened?'

'I dunno. Mix up at the hospital?'

She winks at me. 'It's not like losing your car keys.'

The more I say, the more ridiculous the whole thing becomes in my mind. Maybe I jumped on the drama of it all, and dragged Kane and Shell along for the ride?

Mum's face is hard to read but her eyes are a little watery. I guess I was so busy thinking about myself that I didn't think that this would impact her.

'I don't know what goes through your head sometimes Angus.'

She hands me my phone back and drops the plant down on the table before hobbling inside. The plant's roots are broken and spread across the table in bits.

Suddenly I can't breathe. Why did I bring this up? I'm overwhelmed with the need to hide. My eyes lock on the old cubbyhouse Dad built me when we moved in here, jammed into the corner of the yard. It's not made properly, not square, and nothing quite lines up. The paint on the weatherboards is almost completely gone, and the iron roof is rusted in one corner. The two windows are caked in dust, framed by ragged curtains that Mum made out of an old tablecloth. They have moth holes in them the size of carnival clown mouths. I wonder how long it would take Mum to find me if I hid in there.

Instead, I go and lay on my bed and try to calm myself down. I take deep breaths and listen to an app that plays sounds like a rainstorm in the distance. It helps.

Mum and I don't really speak for the rest of the day and night. I stay in my room, obsessing about our conversation and feeling jittery. I text Shell and Kane but get no response. I need to talk to them. I can feel myself spiralling. I've gotten no answers on anything and hurt Mum in the process. It's like I've opened a door that I'm not sure I can ever close. I feel sick.

Later I sneak back out into the yard with a torch and open the cubbyhouse door, wincing as it creaks loudly. Looking over my shoulder to make sure Mum can't see, I just manage to squeeze through the doorway.

Inside, there is no room to stand so I sit on the floor, legs apart, each foot jammed into opposite corners.

When I was little, the cubby was where I would host tea parties for toys, and write secret invisible ink letters in lemon juice. It was where I read *Harry Potter*, feeling just like Harry, trapped under the stairs waiting for someone to discover I was special.

The only thing inside the cubby is an old wooden box in one corner, roughly the size of a biscuit tin. It's covered in a thick coating of dust that I have to wipe away to open. Inside is an old Swiss Army knife that Dad gave me ages ago. I unwrap it from the soft cloth he kept it in and watch it gleam in the half-light. It has a green handle, rather than the usual red. Dad said it was rare, like me.

Lifting up my shirt, I rub a previous cutting scar on my stomach. I used to cut on the inside of my thighs where no one could see, but I've moved on to the underside of my stomach because it felt better for some reason. I haven't done this in a while . . .

I push the knife in gently, feeling the skin tear. As my skin flares and burns, the pain seeps out of my pores. Release. Something new to feel.

I close my eyes and imagine myself from above. Up there, I look like a broken toy shoved awkwardly into a small, dusty dollhouse. Down here I feel happy in my pain.

Eventually the feeling fades, and I open my eyes. There's blood on my shirt. How weird to be made of such strange jam.

# Chapter 7

# Lawnmower

Sunday morning I lay in bed, feeling the Bandaids pull on my stomach as I breathe. After cutting last night, I felt so calm I was able to get straight to sleep. No racing heart, no fishhooks.

As I get dressed, I make a real effort to think positively about Mum and Dad. All the good stuff I can think of over the years. Birthdays. Games. Stupid jokes.

The first thing I have to do this morning is mow the lawn, like I promised. The sun is already climbing in the sky, but inside the shed, it's gloomy. It takes my eyes a second to adjust before I can see Dad's old orange Victa lawnmower sitting in the corner.

Dad loved his shed, loved buying tools and tinkering with things, despite being terrible at it. Mum and I would roll our eyes as he wobbled on ladders and drilled things, causing just as much damage as he was fixing. Still, at least he tried.

Dad was just awesome. I miss him a lot. When it was the three of us, things were much nicer. We were a family. Mum was different back then too, way more fun.

Dad was really tall, with short dark brown hair, pale freckly skin, and a kind face with a beaky nose. Like Mum, he looked nothing like me.

He was an insurance analyst, which would have been a dull job. I think he wanted a more exciting life, so he was always making stupid plans, like buying a surfboard and paying for surfing lessons that he never went to, or starting an architecture course but not finishing it.

Mum would have to be the bad guy and explain the consequences of his wild plans, like he was a kid who never thought things through, which was kinda true.

One thing he *was* good at was mowing the lawn. Now that he's gone, I mow the way he taught me, in tight rows, so that the grass ends up with this cool striped effect. I always liked the sound of the mower's small engine firing up. Very analogue. As I start up the mower now, that sound connects me to him, like a rope stretching through time.

Mum is nearby, sitting in the shade under the verandah on a banana lounge, her legs elevated. She's sipping water and watching me from under her wide-brimmed sunhat.

'Watch the sprinkler, Gussy!' she calls out as I push the mower too close to the top edge of the lawn.

'Don't worry, I saw it.' I totally didn't.

When I was a kid, sometimes Dad would turn off the mower and let me jump on and ride it around the lawn, while he'd grumble about how heavy I was. Wish I'd done that more with him. You grow out of things like that, not knowing that you'll never get to do them again.

I remember Mum asking me to mow the lawn that weird day five years ago. I must have been ten. It had been early in the morning on a cold day, and we were waiting out the front of the house for a cab. I yawned and steam came out of my mouth like I was a foggy dragon.

Inside the taxi I wiped condensation off the window and flattened my hand against the glass, fingers spread wide. Through my fingers I could see our house, the galvanised iron roof, the white weatherboards, the iced-over windows and the frosty verandah. It looked lonely without Dad. Life in pieces.

Mum turned to me in the back seat. 'I want you to mow the lawn this week. It's time you took on that responsibility now.'

'No way.' That was Dad's job.

'Yes way, Gussy,' she said, smiling sadly.

I just stared into the side mirror, thinking about how, when I was much younger, I was a little obsessed with the peppercorn trees by the railway tunnels. Dad and I would climb to the top of the railway embankment where the purple peppercorn trees were thickest. I loved their spicy aroma and the crunch of fallen seeds under my feet. We'd straddle magic carpets made of flattened cardboard boxes, and then kick off with our feet from the top, sailing down the hill with one arm raised high, cowboy-style, the other gripping a box corner. At the bottom we would crash into the trees, sending leaves and peppercorns flying in all directions. He would always fall off because he was Dad, and because he had crazy long legs. I was fat even back then so it was easier for me to stay on.

In the taxi with Mum, as we went to visit him after the accident, I told her how much I loved those magic carpet rides.

'Remember how Dad would put a peppercorn in his hand and crush it into powder, then blow it in the air? He said it was magic dust.'

'I remember you nearly went blind that one time when it went into your eyes,' she laughed. Then her face hardened. 'He could be stupid.'

'Don't you mean he *can* be stupid?' I'd said, shaking my head at her. I hated that she was already talking about him in the past tense. She went to say something, but instead she closed up like a paper fan.

So there we were, sitting silently as the taxi drove us to the Austin

Hospital, this huge, austere building on the other side of Melbourne. We went up a big lift with doors at both ends (which always seems weird), and walked through to his ward, following the coloured lines on the floor past the nurse's station, nodding hellos like regulars. I hated going there. I hated the way other people on the ward watched Mum's hobbled walk as we passed by.

Dad's room was beige, drab and empty except for a bleeping monitor that sounded like underwater sonar. Very soap opera, but without the hot doctors and nurses.

Mum had brought in some flowers two days ago but they were already nearly dead in the chipped vase. She reached out to them and crushed one between her nicotine-stained fingers.

Cath, the nurse watching Dad that day, looked up.

'Hi Meg. Can you keep an eye on him while I go to the loo, please? I'm busting.'

Mum nodded, and sank awkwardly into the chair by the bed, scratching furiously at her legs through her jeans. I remember her doing everything she could to not actually look directly at his face that morning. She rearranged Dad's things on the side table, threw the flowers in the bin, poured the murky water down the sink, and smoothed the beige blanket over his unmoving legs. Anything to avoid the person in the bed.

After a while she left the room, muttering something about coffee.

Then it was just me and Dad. I looked at his scarred face, bandaged head, and breathing tube snaking out of his mouth. He was so tall his feet hung out one side of the bed.

Just after Mum left the room his eyes suddenly opened. I actually jumped with surprise. He hadn't moved for nearly two weeks. His eyes looked as if they were unsure what being open even meant anymore. There was gunk in the corner of his mouth. I wanted to wipe it away but I didn't.

The wrinkles on his forehead made him seem much older now, and he'd lost weight. His hair was wrong. I didn't realise he dyed it until then. The pale ginger regrowth made him look vulnerable.

But his eyes . . . he just stared at me, unfocused and a bit creepy.

I didn't know what to say. I managed to mumble 'Hi?'

He seemed to be struggling to speak. I leaned in closer to him to hear what he was trying to say, but the breathing tube was in the way. He managed to pull it out.

'Bell,' he muttered, urgently shaking his head as his voice seemed to escape him again.

'Bell?' I was confused. 'You want me to ring the bell for help?' I pushed the emergency buzzer and a nurse arrived almost immediately.

'What's happened? Where's Cath?' the new nurse asked, leaning over and taking his pulse. He had slumped back into his pillows, disappearing back inside himself. She gently moved the breathing tube back into position.

Mum had reappeared with a takeaway coffee. 'What's wrong?' she asked, seeing the nurse fussing over Dad.

The nurse checked Dad's monitors. 'It seems like he woke out of his coma for a moment.'

Mum rushed to Dad's side and grabbed his arm. 'This is a good sign, isn't it?'

The nurse looked to me and then back to Mum. She lowered her voice, but I still heard her. 'We don't want him to wake up yet. We put him in a medical coma to stop him moving about to give his brain injury a chance to heal.'

Mum nodded and sighed. 'Yes, you did tell me that before.'

The nurse gave her a half-smile. 'He's gone back under, so that's good.'

'When he woke up, he stared at me all weird,' I told Mum after the nurse left.

'Did he say anything?' Mum asked sharply.

'No,' I lied. No idea why, but I did.

Mum flopped back into the chair again. She reached into her purse for some change and told me to go get some chips from the vending machine down the hall.

I remember asking what flavour.

'Anything, just go!' she snapped. Why was she angry with me?

I stepped out into the hallway, but then I turned and came back to ask her if I could get a drink too. That's when I saw her leaning over him in the bed, a strange, sad look on her face.

'Are you really awake?' she asked. No response. She grabbed his hand. 'I want to breathe in your last breath and taste forgiveness on it.'

I must have gasped. She looked up at me guiltily, like I'd caught her stealing out of his wallet or something. I will never forget that moment. What did she mean about forgiveness?

Mum rubbed her eyes and gestured to me. I went over to her and she put her arms around me. 'He'll be alright, you'll see. We'll all be alright.'

He died later that day, after we'd left, from a cerebral bleed.

\* \* \*

'Are you okay?'

I realise I am standing in the middle of the lawn with my hands on the mower's handle, shaking as the motor turns over and vibrates through my arms. I must have been so deep in my head that I stopped moving entirely. What did Dad want to tell me that day?

And what about Mum? At the time I thought she was asking him for forgiveness for the car accident, but what if it was something else?

I turn to her. What is she not telling me? Mum stares back at me. I wonder if the glass by her chair is filled with vodka, not water.

*Shut up!* Now I'm just making up stuff to suit the story in my head.

# Chapter 8

# Pool

Monday after school I go to Kane's place, as usual. He is sitting on the edge of his bed, doing arm curls with a huge dumbbell. *Doctor Who* is playing in the background on TV, of course, the episode where Weeping Angels have trapped everyone in a house. He's clearly not coping well with all this time on his hands.

I watch his biceps expand as he pumps the weight up and down. I don't know how he can be bothered. I get tired just watching him.

'Hey Goose. What's new?'

'Nothing really.'

Kane puts his dumbbell down and looks at me. 'Been spiralling about that website, have you?'

I nod. He knows me well.

'There's nothing to worry about mate. It doesn't mean anything,' he says.

'Yeah, of course, I know that. But what if there's a tiny, tiny chance?'

'Okay, sure, but what makes you think that?'

How do I explain it when I don't even understand it myself? There's just this nagging doubt that I can't shake.

'I don't really know, but I don't feel like I fit in anywhere.'

'Why? 'Cos you're fat, do you mean?'

'No, but thanks for the fat shaming.'

'Sorry, I just meant—'

'I know what you meant. No, it's not that. It's like when Mum got glasses for the first time a few years back. She was walking round the house saying stuff like, "Oh, now I understand why Tom never liked those curtains".'

Kane looks at me blankly.

'All I mean is I've always felt like I didn't fit into my family, but I didn't know why. It's like there's something I wasn't seeing because I didn't have the right glasses, or something?'

'Mate, with my buggered knee, I don't seem to fit in with the footy guys anymore either. I mean, who am I if I'm not a footy legend?' He stares at me seriously, then grins.

'Shut up, that's temporary. I've always felt like this. I don't look like Mum or Dad and there's weird stuff like my parents not having any baby photos of me, and we have no other relatives, no cousins, no uncles or aunties, no grandparents. What are the chances?'

'Okay, it's strange, sure. But there's a difference between having an odd family situation and being a kidnapped kid.'

He's right. There could be a hundred explanations. 'I know. It's just this feeling I can't shake. Like I'm meant to be someone else, somewhere else.'

'Who? Where?'

I raise my hands in an 'I don't know' gesture and slump down on the sofa. Kane awkwardly hobbles from the bed to sit down too. I try to focus on the episode but I'm barely taking it in, although watching the Doctor turning into a stone angel is distracting me a bit.

I turn to him. 'I showed Mum the pic and she said it wasn't me.'

'Woah. So how did she take it? Was she upset or angry?'

'She kinda laughed it off, but I felt like it struck a nerve, so I kept pushing. But I didn't get anything more. I could tell that she was hurt, so I left it.'

Kane nods, his face softening. 'Hey, I get that she might be funny about it, but you should be able to ask her questions. It's not like you're asking for money for new footy boots. This is a big deal.'

Like I would ask for footy anything! He's right though.

'Anyway, it could be worse. Look at me. No girlfriend, no footy, busted knee, no proper job, working at Macca's part time . . . everything's a bit shit right now.'

'No apprenticeships out there?'

'No apprenticeships anywhere. Got my name down at McMullens down on Rathdowne Road, and that engineering place near the old brewery.'

'What about the mechanic near the pool?'

Kane doesn't respond; he shuffles back to the bed and starts curling again.

* * *

Kane's energy has always been endless and exhausting. It's like his arms and legs are divining rods, drawing strength straight from the ground. Before his injury he used to come tearing up his driveway at me like a whirlwind, leaping on my back and yelling something sporty.

When Kane was fifteen, he became captain of the local under sixteen footy team. There were photos of him smiling, all teeth and trophies, in the local paper and on socials. And why not? He was a great full-forward, fit, good-looking and even blond. All the girls wanted him, all the boys wanted to be him – the true teen movie cliché.

He dropped out halfway through VCE last year, saying he was sick of school and was probably going to fail anyway. At first he blamed the pandemic, but then he said school was like a boring movie he wanted to walk out of. He wanted to get a job and to focus on sport.

Then he busted up his knee, which meant a reconstruction and lots of physio. That was footy done for this season, and maybe the next.

While he may have escaped school, suddenly he was facing another boring movie: unemployment. He spent months applying for apprenticeships with no luck. He applied to the local gym, but they wanted people with fitness qualifications. He even tried to get a job at a cafe, but they wanted someone with barista or hospo experience. After all these rejections, I suggested he apply at Macca's.

'They're desperate for workers right now. Two people got sacked last week for stealing.'

'What would you steal from there? Nuggets?'

'A job is a job. It's not a bad place to work.'

'It's a shithole. No way. Kids who work there get stuck on a road to nowhere for life.'

'Got any better options?'

He started the following week.

Working with Kane is awesome. I've been at Macca's a whole three months longer and I get to show him the ropes, so for once in my life I am better at something than him, other than reading and like, school in general, I guess. It won't last but I am totally milking it for all it's worth.

He fit in really well right from the start. He bounces about, flipping meat patties in the air like he's working in some New York burger joint. Meanwhile I mostly just stand there bored, pushing timer buttons and loading chicken nuggets into deep fryers. Sometimes we fling fries at one another and get into trouble with one of the high school dropout managers. As a punishment, we get sent to the car park to pick up rubbish or to the playground to clean up vomit.

Until his injury, he used to bang on about sport and fitness. When he talked about Carlton, or just footy in general, his eyes would burn with passion, like it was his calling. He described how his fingers connect to the seams when he holds a footy, and how his arms and legs work in unison for the perfect punt.

I used to get sick of him talking about footy. But now he barely mentions it at all, which seems even sadder. It's like a door has closed for him, a door that was meant to lead somewhere important.

Luckily Mum made me get swimming lessons when I was younger or I would be a total sports dud. Of course, I dreaded every session at first, feeling awkward in my unflattering swim shorts. Once I got over all that, I actually ended up being a pretty strong swimmer. Finally I had something I was good at, one thing that was mine.

A couple of years back, a few of the older guys from Kane's footy team signed up for this local under eighteen half triathlon. They signed Kane up too, assuming he'd do it. The running and the cycling would be a breeze for him. But not the swimming.

Kane always shudders when I mention being underwater. He told me once that every time he puts his head under, he imagines his skeleton is being crushed, his heart bursting, his lungs starved of oxygen, his eyes bulging like an exploding fish.

'It's so weird that you can't swim when you're so good at everything else,' I'd said when he mentioned the triathlon.

Kane glared back at me. 'You can't even kick a footy! Easiest thing in the world.'

'Swimming is easier.'

'Mum and Dad can't swim either,' Kane added, as if it was somehow genetic.

'In a way, swimming is like footy – it's all about your arms and legs finding the right rhythm.'

Kane's eyes opened wide. I was quite pleased with that analogy.

'Maybe we could teach each other?' I suggested.

So we made a pact for the coming weekend. He would teach me how to kick a footy and I would teach him how to swim. What could go wrong?

By the time Sunday rolled around, kicking a football was the last thing I wanted to do, but we'd made a deal.

We met in the railway park over the road in the morning. He was in his Carlton guernsey and shorts, all ready. He started with handballing the ball to me, trying to get me used to its size and shape. I was okay at that, sort of. But then we moved on to kicking. Kane showed me the motions, how to hold the ball, at what point I should aim my foot – but I stuffed it up every time. He stood there shaking his head. It was humiliating, especially when I saw Mum and Fiona 'gardening' out the front, no doubt keeping an eye out on this unusual event.

'C'mon, try harder!' Kane snapped.

*This is all I've got*, I thought to myself, as I failed to kick straight, *again*. Red-faced through exertion and embarrassment, I threw up my hands. 'I give up.'

Our worlds swapped when we went to the pool. Just walking through the gates, I noticed Kane's posture seemed to sink and his face turned this pale grey colour. I'd never seen him like this before.

Of course he looked good in boardies, while I was hiding my whole body in a massive towel. Most of my cuts were on the inside of my legs back then, so my shorts covered them.

It was a hot day, and the pool was busy and noisy. We waited until the deep end was mainly free of kids before we waded in. Over the next hour, no matter what I did, no matter how slowly we went, the minute Kane's head went under he would panic. He'd emerge, staccato-breathed, his short hair plastered to his head in a wet skull-cap. His big arms just didn't seem to work in the pool. They were floppy and uncertain. I had to hold him up in the water, arms around his waist, promising not to let him go. Frustrated, I decided to test the old sink or swim theory with him. I was holding Kane in the water, but not as close to the edge as normal. Suddenly I let go, just like that. Took my arms away and left him to his own devices, just for a moment.

Kane immediately panicked. He spluttered and started to sink. He swallowed a fair bit of water and came up red and choking, looking shit-scared. He went under again and I started to panic too, seeing he was in real trouble. He fought me when I tried to grab him, but eventually I was able to get hold of him properly, and bring him to the surface. I tilted his head and swam him to the edge. Then I got out and got my arms under his shoulders behind him and pulled his big heavy body out of the water. I laid him down on the hot pavement and tilted his head back to clear his air passage and started to give him mouth-to-mouth, just like they showed us in school.

Moments later he spluttered up some water. He tried to sit up but flopped back down. Then came these big tears that galloped out of his bloodshot eyes. He looked vulnerable and weak, two words I'd never thought would fit Kane.

'You promised me you wouldn't let go!' he whimpered, avoiding my gaze.

I muttered that I was sorry.

He sat up and looked me in the eye. 'You can never tell anyone, understand?'

'Of course.'

He stood up and walked off without looking back, collecting his towel and bag on his way. Having me see him like that must have cost him a lot. I felt as if I had peeled off his skin and looked at the threads that held him together.

And that was the end of it. He never had another swimming lesson with me, and I never learned to kick a football. We never spoke about it again. The next day it was like nothing had ever happened. Our friendship never changed. I had hurt him but saved his life at the same time. I had seen him at his lowest. But even in his state, he knew that I'd enjoyed giving him mouth-to-mouth a bit too much. So we kept each other's secrets.

# Chapter 9

# Brush

On Wednesday, I decide that I need to take this kidnap theory out of my head and put it onto paper. My brain won't let it go otherwise. I'm in my room, setting up an investigation timeline with sticky-taped photos and dates on post-its, just like on TV. I've printed out articles and photos and a map of Bellanta I found online, and blu-tacked everything to the back of the wardrobe, which I can easily move away from the wall as it has small wheels. When I'm in here I can just slide the wardrobe around and add things to the timeline. All I need to do is remember to turn it back around before I leave so Mum doesn't see it.

When I first googled the case, I found so many articles about the case, but they all repeated the same information, like the police had put out a media release. I feel like I need to see local *Bellanta Courier* reports from the case over time to see the full picture. I'll have to go to the State Library and track down the actual papers, old school-style. I'm particularly interested in finding out more about Detective Frank Firelli. His name keeps coming up as the local cop leading the investigation, till detectives from Sydney came along and took over. Looks like he was taken off the case. I wonder why. Did he not make enough progress, or do they always bring in city cops for a major crime like kidnapping? I wonder if he is still a detective?

Eventually I find a reference to him being present at a local police event in Bellanta a few years back. There's a photo of him in uniform handing a trophy to a local rookie. Just the sort of thing I want to win one day. He looks grumpy in a fifty-year-old-man way. After some deep googling I also find some vague reference about him buying a farm on the outskirts of Bellanta called Parkhurst. I find the address, but no phone number of course. I make a note of it anyway. It might be worth following up at some point.

The other name that comes up a bit is Mark Reynolds, Jane's ex-boyfriend. There's no pictures of him, but various mentions of him as a suspect. He was never arrested, so they mustn't have had much of a case. There are vague references to other suspects, but none of them are named. This seems weird, but I guess if none of them were arrested either then their names wouldn't be released. I still can't find anything on what happened to Jane Winter.

Suddenly I hear a noise in the hallway and my door flings open. I jump up and push the wardrobe back against the wall to hide the timeline, but it's only Shell.

'It's just me, chill,' she says, barging in. 'How're things going?' She sits on the chair at my desk, swivelling back and forth like she's on *The Apprentice*.

I turn the wardrobe back out to reveal the timeline. 'Um, I'm busy doing a bit of detective work actually.'

'Wow, so you've started without me?' she says, looking over the timeline. 'I know I didn't know your dad, but I really can't see your mum as a kidnapper.'

'Me either, but she sure is acting real strange.'

'I get you want to look into it. We all have stuff that bothers us.'

I'm not sure how to respond. 'Well, it's good to confront things . . .' I say in a 'I-know-what-you're-really-talking-about' kind of way.

'Is that your psych talking?' she asks, one eyebrow raised in a way that I wish I could do.

I laugh, then point to the timeline. 'Anyway, these are the main dates.'

**Timeline**
- Mum and Dad meet in 2006
- Robin is born 20 November 2007
- I'm born 20 December 2007
- Robin kidnapped Monday 1 March 2010
- Break-in at house in Hazleton late 2010
- Car accident October 2018
- Dad dies November 2018
- Find Robin on website November 2023

'Okay, so where do we begin? What leads do we have?' Shell rubs her hands together, eager to get started.

'I keep wondering why there are no family photos from when I was young. Is this break-in story just a cover-up?' I say.

'Maybe they just lost them and don't want to admit it? People tell lies all the time to make themselves look better.'

'Dunno, maybe? It feels like anything is possible right now. It's all so crazy.'

'Ooh, speaking of crazy, I have something to show you.' She reaches into her pocket and takes out a shiny red credit card, waving it in front of me. 'Cheryl gave me this last night. It's her way of getting me to buy more feminine clothes. She literally said I look like a boy, and that I should buy myself some prettier things. Like she's never met me! But I didn't fight her since it meant getting my own card.'

'That's not like you,' I say.

She unleashes a semi-death stare. 'I'll use the card for whatever I want. I dress for me, and I don't need to justify that to her,' she says firmly. 'And if I choose to wear tons of black and look like a punk or a butch then too bad.'

'Totally!' I say.

Shell tucks the card back into her pocket. 'Anyway. Have you decided if you'll show your mum the website?'

'I showed her already.'

'You did? How did she react?'

'She brushed it off and denied the photo looked like me.'

'What? But it does *so* look like you.'

'I know, right?' I say, scratching my stomach.

Her face changes and she stares into my eyes, right into my brain. 'You want it to be true, and that's making you sad.'

'I don't know, maybe?' She's right of course. But why would I want that?

'Wouldn't you remember a thing like this though? If Robin was two or three when he was taken, that's old enough to remember at least something, isn't it? I still kinda remember my second birthday because Larry dressed up like a dinosaur.'

'Maybe I repressed it?'

Shell twists one of the chunky silver rings on her finger. 'Maybe. Did you believe your mum?'

'Not really. She laughed it off, but there's other things that don't add up.' I sit up and start counting on my fingers. 'There's no photos of me as a baby. None before I was about four. No family resemblance to Mum or Dad. No cousins or grandparents on either side . . .'

Shell pulls at a hole in her tights. 'That must be weird. Even though Cheryl drives me nuts with her girly positivity, and Larry is money-obsessed, at least I *look* like both of them. I guess that's somehow comforting.'

'Plus, I've been thinking about the day Dad died. Something he said in the hospital.'

Shell leans in, excited. 'What did he say?'

'One word. "Bell".'

'What?' She sits back, disappointed.

'He had a head injury and was in a medical coma for nearly two weeks, so I just thought he was rambling. But there was something about the way that he said it, like he had something big to tell me . . .'

We seem to have the exact same thought at the exact same time.

'Bellanta!' we blurt in unison.

'What if that's what he meant?'

Shell clasps her hands together. 'It's a theory. So, let's start to build our case. Do you have a birth certificate?'

'I guess so. Everyone does, don't they?'

'Find it. It's a legal document, so it has to have the truth on it. Like your birth parents, or whatever.'

She's right. 'Okay, good start, but there must be other stuff I can do?'

'I was on this online forum the other night and someone was asking if gender fluidity was inherited . . . like you could tell from a DNA test or something.'

'Can you?' I ask.

'No idea. But they were saying that DNA tests are easy to do now, so if your birth certificate isn't useful, you could take a test to see if you're related to your mum.'

'True. Plus, if the police have DNA from Robin from back then my results could change everything.'

This could be huge. My mind kicks into overdrive again. 'I'm not sure if I should do this. What if Mum's actually not my mum?'

'It'll be fine.'

I let out a long breath. 'What would you do if you were me?'

'Well, I'd investigate a bit more. Start the DNA thing.'

She grabs my laptop and shoves it at me. I take it and start googling.

'There's loads of different types of test kits,' I turn the laptop screen to face Shell. 'This place sells a maternity test. That'd work.'

Shell eyes the site. 'Wow, is it that easy?'

I nod. 'Looks like it. All I need is a few of Mum's hairs, and some of my own for comparison. You bung them in separate bags and send them off and they test them to see if we're a genetic match. You can get the results within five days. All for a hundred and forty bucks.'

Suddenly I'm deflated. 'Even if I wanted to do this, Mum would never agree to a test.'

Shell smiles innocently. 'So don't tell her.'

Even talking about this feels like such a betrayal, but I still feel the need to know the truth. 'That's a big deception.'

Shell nods. 'Yes, but she's not telling you the truth either, so . . .'

'Maybe I'll just wait to find the birth certificate first and see what that says?'

'Or you could send off for this DNA test anyway, to be extra sure?'

As usual, she wins me over. 'I guess I could at least order it.' I already feel guilty about this, but I want answers, good or bad. This doesn't mean I'd want her to stop being my mother.

'If she finds out she'll kill me.'

Shell rolls her eyes. 'She won't find out. Send the test to Kane's place. New topic now: I'm thinking of shaving all my hair off, what do you think?'

Her attempt at distracting me is not subtle, but probably a good idea.

'Sure, but why?'

'I want to explore looking a bit different, maybe piss Mum off a bit more. And also all this black dye has made my hair so brittle it's starting to fall out.'

'Do it,' I say. 'A new you.'

'Not a new me, but a more "me" me.' She smiles.

I get what she means, I think.

* * *

After I see Shell to the door, I head into the lounge room. Mum is laying on the couch with her legs elevated on the armrest. She has a glass of wine by her side and a smoke in her hand. She's watching some trashy reality show where hot, dumb people are screaming banal shit at one another.

'These people are vile,' she says, enjoying every minute of it.

I don't know what to say to her. I can't just demand my birth certificate. She knows how to shut me down.

'If only they cared about something important, like climate change,' I mutter.

'Well that would be a worthy but dull show. Anyway, what did Shell want?' Mum asks.

She's made it easy for me. 'We're doing this assignment for science. I, um, need my birth certificate.'

She glances up at me with a strange look on her face. 'Why?'

'We have to do our family tree.'

'You don't need a birth certificate to do your family tree,' she says evenly. Her mouth is a flat slit.

'They said we do.'

'Well, you don't have one, so you'll just have to tell your teacher that you can't do the assignment.'

I wasn't expecting this. 'Why? Did you lose it along with all my baby photos?'

'No, Angus. I don't want to talk about this anymore. Please leave it.' She sounds annoyed and tired at the same time.

Deflated, I turn around and walk back down the corridor to my room.

I lay on the bed and listen to my calming noises app with my eyes closed, the volume turned all the way up to drown out the thoughts in my head.

About an hour later I'm suddenly aware of someone else in the room. I open my eyes to find Mum standing over me, wine glass still in hand, saying something I can't hear. I take off my headphones.

'Did you like growing up in this house?' She's slurring her words a bit. Great, she's pissed.

'Sorry?'

'Did you have a good childhood? Were you taken care of? Were you fed? Taken to school? Looked after?'

'Yes.' *What is this about?*

She points a finger at me, wine sloshing in her glass. 'Then that's all you need to know.'

'I have questions, that's all,' I say. 'And that photo looks so much like me.'

'This house, this room, this life, isn't it enough?' She gestures around her.

'But—'

'Dad and I loved you and cared for you and kept you safe. You don't need a birth certificate to tell you that. The fact that you're here, alive, tells you that. And I know that the accident ripped our lives apart in the most awful way. But we survived.'

'Mum . . .' my voice cracks and I can feel my eyes stinging.

She sighs. 'Leave it, Angus. Has Shell put you up to this? I'll be calling Cheryl if she has.'

'No. But I've always felt wrong somehow.'

She rubs her hand up and down the back of her neck, her voice getting louder. 'You kids think life should be shiny all the time. That's not real.' She points to her legs. 'We lost Dad. Everything changed. But you and I are still here and that's what's real.'

She stops shouting and the anger slides away from her face like melting ice cream.

She speaks quietly. 'Look, you are my son. I want you to be happy. Leave this alone and you will be happier.'

She gets up slowly and hobbles out of my room.

My heart is racing. I can feel myself on the edge of a panic attack, so I head to the bathroom to get a drink of water. Knocking it back settles my heart a bit, but I'm still jittery. I go to refill my glass and there it is: her hairbrush sitting next to the basin. I pull a few hairs from the brush and wrap them in a tissue. Then I pull out some of my own hairs and wrap them in a different tissue. Cradling both hair bundles, I head back to my room and text Kane about getting the DNA test kit sent to his flat under his name.

The real investigation begins tomorrow.

# Chapter 10

# Wheelbarrow

When I was a kid, I used to follow Mum and Dad around like a puppy. Dad used to call me their little shadow. I loved being close to them. Mum always smelled like perfume and bleach – the soft prettiness of one and the hard cleanliness of the other. She still does, under a layer of wine and stale cigarette smoke. Dad smelled like musty aftershave.

One night, not long before the accident, something changed. I was maybe ten. Mum was out somewhere, no idea where. I think I'd asked Dad once or twice but he brushed me off, which wasn't like him. I knew they had been arguing. I kept looking to the door for her because I had just finished making a model police car out of Lego that I wanted to show her. Dad said it was great, but I wanted her opinion too.

He let me stay up watching TV with him. I remember sitting on the floor in front of his chair, with his big feet either side of me, scratching my birthmarks.

'Stop scratching. You got fleas?'

'No!'

'It's time for you and your fleas to go to bed,' he smiled. I gave him five reasons why I needed to stay up. I can't remember what they were, but at the time they were totally valid.

'Ten more minutes and I'll go, promise,' I begged, but he was having none of it.

He pointed me toward the door. I pretended to clean my teeth (but really only swirled some toothpaste in my mouth) and went to bed. I lay awake, ears straining to hear Mum coming through the front door.

When he came to check on me, I pretended to be asleep. I remember him turning off my lamp and closing my door. Once he was gone again, I snuck out of bed and peeked through the not-quite-shut lounge door. I expected to see him still watching TV, but he was just sitting there, staring at his phone, looking sad or mad – I couldn't tell. Suddenly he jumped to his feet. I just managed to hide behind my door in time as he walked past my room and into the bathroom.

While he was in the bathroom, I snuck a look at his phone. He had sent heaps of texts to Mum, saying stuff like 'Where are you?', 'Are you okay?', 'How drunk are you?'. One text after the other, each one a bit sadder than the one before.

When I heard the toilet flush, I ran back to bed.

I must have dozed for a while because the next thing I remember is jumping awake at the sound of the front door banging. I thought it was Mum coming home, so I pulled on my dressing gown and slippers, grabbed my police car, and ran into the hallway, but it was actually Dad leaving the house, shining a torch ahead of him.

Even then I was a good detective and took note of the time: 1.30 am.

Something inside me really wanted to find out what was going on, so I snuck out after him, even though I was worried that he'd be angry. I stayed at a distance, in the shadows, just like on TV. There weren't lots of lights in our street, but the moon and his torch lit the way for me. He shone his torch everywhere as he walked down the street: front yards, gutters, driveways.

His steps were heavy. I could tell he was angry.

Then he headed toward the railway line and the stormwater tunnels. The tunnels scared me. They were always dark, even in the middle of the day, so I would always hold Mum or Dad's hand tight if we walked through them.

Dad stood at the mouth of the first tunnel and shone his torch down its throat like he was a dentist looking for a cavity. 'Megan?' he called out. No answer. He moved to the second tunnel.

'Shit!' He ran in.

I followed. He'd stopped a metre or so into the tunnel, and was bent over Mum, who was laying on the ground, covered in mud. She looked wet and broken, like a toy dropped into a puddle. Dad was shaking her and wiping her mouth. There was a pile of spew on the ground near her.

'Mum!' I called out in panic.

Dad spun around to me in shock. He scrambled over to me and grabbed my shoulders.

'Gussy, what are you doing out of bed? Go home!'

I didn't answer. I was trying to get to Mum. Even though I was scared, I still had to know what was wrong with her.

'Mum is a bit sick,' he said, 'Stay here.' He let go of me and turned back to Mum.

'What's wrong with her?' I asked. He glared at me for not doing as I was told, but then his face softened, and he started explaining that we needed to help her home.

He bent to lift her up and cried out in agony, clutching his back. He tried to straighten up but he seemed to be stuck in a hunch.

His yelling must have woken her up. She was mumbling and waving her arms at him. He tried again to lift her but she started slapping him. 'Stop it,' he said, really angry now. She kept going, slapping him over and over.

'Mum, what's wrong?' I went in to help her up.

'Gus, you can't be here.' Dad pulled me away, grunting.

We headed home, leaving Mum in the tunnel.

When we got back, Dad headed straight to the shed. He suddenly seemed different, more determined. I stood in the doorway as he pulled an old picnic blanket off his wheelbarrow.

'Your mother isn't well, so we're going to help her,' he said as he dusted the wheelbarrow down.

'What's wrong with her?' I asked through tears. He didn't answer. I wanted him to let me help, so I didn't ask again.

We walked back to the tunnel with the wheelbarrow. Dad pushed it, nose down, toward Mum, trying to scoop her up. Slowly, carefully.

'C'mon, help me out here.' But she didn't move.

Dad grit his teeth as he lifted her up again for another try. 'One . . . two . . .'

Eventually he got her in, and we wheeled her home. Despite his back, he pushed the wheelbarrow firmly, weaving around so that we were in shadow, not lit by streetlights.

Looking back, I realise that he let me see something I could never forget.

A few days later we had the car accident. Dad died, Mum's legs were damaged . . . and I walked away without a scratch. Dr Yamada says the reasons I started cutting are control and guilt.

# Chapter 11

# Kit

The next day Kane sends me a text.

> *Got message saying test kit will come by*
> *end of day*

Shit, that was quick. I don't know what I'm going to do once I get the results. Hopefully they'll say I'm related to Mum and then I can forget all about this. But what if the results say we're not related? Then what do I do? Whatever happens, I feel like she's hiding something. What she said about the birth certificate felt like a lie, but I don't know how to prove it. Even though she's being weird, it doesn't mean my kidnap theory is true.

If only I could remember more about my childhood. I have always felt a bit separate to Mum and Dad, this house, everything. It's like there's been a curtain between me and the world for as long as I can remember. But now each piece of this Robin Winter story I discover is a knife that rips another hole in that curtain.

My mind is like a Catherine wheel firework, shooting sparks in all directions. I am distracted all day at school by all these ideas swirling in my head. I just need to put them into some kind of order. This heatwave isn't helping either.

I rush home from school and dump my bag on the bed. I'm just about to roll the wardrobe away from the wall when there's a knock at my door.

'Open up Gussy.'

Mum! She walks in, carrying a bunch of shirts and jeans, and heads toward the wardrobe. Just before she opens the wardrobe door, she stops and stares at my room.

'Have you been moving the furniture around?'

I panic. 'Yes, just mixing things up.'

She looks at me funny, but she turns back and starts putting my shirts away without saying anything. As she pulls out a drawer, a piece of paper from the timeline falls to the floor. My heart stops.

She's busy putting away my jeans and doesn't notice. It's the picture of Robin. I jump up to help her, kicking the paper under my bed.

She smiles at me. 'Do you have much homework this weekend? I thought we could spend some time together. Get a pizza. Watch a movie or something.'

'I'm staying at Shell's Saturday night. We have to come up with an idea for a Business Studies project.' It's a half-lie. I have actually arranged to stay at Shell's, but it's to go through every bit of the case with her properly. Her eagle eye will help me wade through everything I've found.

'Okay then.' She sounds disappointed.

We both stare at each other. Lots to say, but we don't speak. That's how we roll these days.

The doorbell rings, and the awkward moment ends.

'That'll be Kane,' I say.

She leaves the room without saying a word. I hear her talking to him at the front door. It's hard to hear clearly, but it sounds like something about physio or a pool or something.

Kane comes into my room and closes the door. He silently passes me the testing kit package, a box the size of a fat novel. I rip it open and start sorting through the swabs, blank labels, and a sheet of instructions to find the sealable plastic bags I need. The hair samples I took the other day are in a box under my bed. I pull the box from its hiding place, and carefully put Mum's sample in one bag and mine in the other. Then I fill out the info on the labels, attach them to the bags and slide them into the provided return post envelope.

I wave it at Kane. 'I put your address on it again, hope that's okay. I'll post it today.'

'Sure, whatever you need. You're enjoying this, aren't you?'

I ignore this. 'Text me when you get the results please? Should only take five days.'

'Course.'

I tell Mum we're going next door, but we actually walk down the road to the letterbox at the end of the street.

'Want me to make sure we're not under surveillance?' Kane jokes, hiding behind the letterbox, his big feet sticking out in clear view. I roll my eyes.

The next few days are gonna be long.

* * *

Shell's house is on the other side of Hazleton. It's a much nicer part of the suburb than mine and Kane's: near the golf course, far from the railway line. Her house is huge, with a fancy front door, double garage, and a manicured yard with a pool they never use. It makes my house look small and ordinary, which it kinda is. I ring the doorbell and instantly Mrs Oliver is there, all big eyes, big hair, warm smile, arms open wide to welcome me. She's wearing a pink scarf around her head, an asymmetrical pink-and-white shirt, and silky, flowing pants. She looks stylish and rich. She smells rich too, like the perfume counter at David Jones.

'Gus, come in, come in,' she almost sings, grabbing me in a bear hug. I can't imagine Mum greeting one of my friends like this. I mean, she's friendly enough, but in a distant kind of way.

'Stop it, Cheryl!' Shell's voice comes from down the hall. 'You are super embarrassing.'

Shell is almost a clone of her mother – the same height, same shape, same face – apart from their age, the only difference is Shell's ripped black clothes and spiky black hair compared to Cheryl's pink clothes and sleekly styled blonde hair. I used to joke that she was Shell's future, which usually earned me a punch to my arm or a kick to my shin.

We spend the night watching trash on the big TV that's mounted to the wall in Shell's room. Unlike the rest of the stylish, white Hamptons-inspired house, her room is decorated with black wallpaper. The room is a mess, with clothes and shoes and schoolwork scattered everywhere. The only neat thing is the bookcase, which is full of books on crime and climate change and environmental issues. Lately she's been vibing Greta Thunberg.

We kinda lose track of things in this black room, out of step with time altogether, like at the movies. Periodically her mum pops her head through the door, asking if we're hungry. The answer is yes, always.

I tell Shell all the latest: Mum acting strange, my 'missing' birth certificate, and the arrival of the DNA kit. 'I just don't believe her.'

Shell laps it up. 'Your life just got way more interesting.'

She's good at backhanded compliments like that. You smile at first and then you think, *Oh hang on . . .*

'When will you get the DNA results?'

'I should have an answer by Thursday next week. The waiting is already driving me nuts and it's only been a few hours.'

'This will help distract you. I found this great new crime series.'

She hands me a book to look over. We're a good match, when it comes to a detective partnership. I'm into crime scene investigation and forensics, whereas she's more into the psychological aspects of crimes and why the person did it. Two halves of a whole.

'So, any closer to talking to your parents about the gender stuff?'

Shell looks a bit uncomfortable. 'No. It's not that simple,' she says, waving a pack of Cheezels in front of me. 'Want one?' I grab a handful and sneak a glance at her.

Her face is still, her eyes watchful. She opens her mouth but then closes it again, saying nothing. Shell being quiet is a rare, almost unsettling thing. It looks like a bunch of emotions are flashing across her face. Finally she speaks.

'You know how you say you don't feel like you belong in your family sometimes?'

'. . . Yeah?'

'Well I'm feeling a bit like that as well. Like I belong somewhere else. Not in the wrong family, but maybe . . . in the wrong body for who I'm meant to be.'

'You mean non-binary?'

'Maybe, maybe not. Some days I feel I'm more male than female, then other days it's the other way round.'

She stares at me, her big dark eyes looking lost.

'Oh, so you're gender queer?'

'God, Gus! Stop trying to put a label on it. I'm not a problem to solve.' She folds her arms over her chest. 'Forget it. Let's just watch something, but not *Doctor Who*.'

She grabs the remote. I go to speak but realise it's better to keep my mouth shut on this topic. I feel like I have let her down.

'Can we watch *Love, Simon* again?' I ask.

\* \* \*

The next morning I wake up bloated after having eaten my body weight in Cheezels last night. I drag myself out of the spare room bed, get dressed and stick my head through Shell's doorway. I want to clear the air about last night, but she's snoring like a beast, so I close the door again.

Shell's mum is in the kitchen, standing in front of their huge, top-of-the-range coffee machine, looking puzzled. 'Would you like a coffee, Gus? You'll just need to give me a minute, I'm still trying to get the hang of this thing.'

'No thanks, I'm good.'

She stares at the machine. 'My girl still asleep?'

'Yes, snoring away.'

She laughs. 'It runs in the family.' Then she turns to me properly. 'Please don't tell her I asked you this, but is she okay? She's not been herself lately. Withdrawn. Really crabby.'

'She seems fine to me,' I say. Like I'd be saying anything about Shell behind her back.

She doesn't look like she believes me. She's rubbing her manicured hands together, her nails making scratching sounds against each other. 'You'd let me know if anything was wrong, wouldn't you?'

It's not really a question, it's a statement. Cheryl is usually such a bubbly, positive person, so I'm a bit thrown by this.

'Of course.' It's not like I can say no.

I say goodbye, leaving her frowning at the giant coffee machine.

As I ride my bike home, I wonder about Shell. I've come out as gay to her, but last night was the closest she ever came to talking to me about her sexuality. She vibes as gay, but questioning her gender is new. I've been so caught up in this Robin Winter case that I've not been paying enough attention to her. I feel like a shitty friend.

When I come through the back door, Mum gives me a weird smile where her mouth is smiling but her eyes aren't. I realise that she would have had to do her stockings alone this morning. I'm letting everyone down at the moment.

'Did you get your Business Studies project done last night?'

'Not really.'

She runs her fingers through her hair and I notice that her hand seems a little shaky. 'Maybe we can spend some time together tonight then?' she asks tentatively.

'Sure.' I walk past her to my room.

* * *

After school I keep looking online for more articles or reports about Robin's kidnapping. If I do find something, it's just more of the same info over and over, nothing new. Jane Winter was distraught. Mark Reynolds was a suspect but never arrested. Detective Firelli was calling out for information from the local community – surely someone must have seen something. I read a couple of articles that talk about police divers searching the creek that runs near the house where Robin was taken from, looking for a body. Creepy.

The *Bellanta Courier*'s website is useless, with the archive function barely searchable, so I ring them up directly and speak to some girl who sounds bored to be alive. I tell her I'm doing a big assignment for school and need access to old papers. She says if I can get to Bellanta, I can go through their archives. She takes my details. I don't know if I'll go through with this, since Bellanta is in New South Wales, but at least it feels like a move forward.

Waiting days for these DNA results is killing me. Why can't it be like a pregnancy test? You piss on a stick and wait a few minutes or whatever, then boom, you have the results? (And your life changes forever . . . or not.) Still, while I wait, I can try to spend a bit more time figuring out if I can help Shell. I don't want her to feel like she's wrong, in her body or in the world.

# Chapter 12

# Torana

The next few days drag on forever, like a TV show with way too many episodes and not enough happening. Even though I try to focus on other things, Robin Winter is always at the back of my mind. And waiting for the DNA results make me feel like I'm in limbo, trapped between an unclear past and an unknown future.

Wednesday afternoon Shell and I skip Advanced Science and catch a train into the city. The plan is to visit the State Library. I'm hoping the train ride will give us a chance to talk properly after the other night's awkwardness. The carriage is fairly empty, which makes sense given it's the middle of the day in the middle of the week.

Shell sits opposite me and is in a chatty mood. She rests her combat boots up on the seat next to me. 'Does your mum know you're not at school?'

'No.'

Shell snickers. 'She'll blame me for this, I bet. She doesn't like me much.' It's like a question, but not.

'She thinks you're fine.' I say, without meeting her eye.

'*Fine*? Oooh shit, she must hate me then!'

'No,' I awkwardly stutter, 'she just . . .' I trail off.

'What? Tell me.'

I sigh. 'She thinks you're a strong influence on me.'

'Does she now.' Shell turns her death stare on full beam.

'Whatever. I don't think that's a bad thing, right?' I say.

'Doesn't she think you have a mind of your own?'

'She still treats me like a kid, so . . .' I look at my phone and change the subject unconvincingly. 'The library should have papers from all around Australia on their online database or on microfilm, whatever that is.'

We both look out the window and don't really talk. I can feel her anger bubbling away opposite me.

We get off at Melbourne Central station and get on the escalator to go up to street level. Shell is stomping ahead of me. She stomps when she's angry, like Dad used to. There's an awkward silence as we cross the road and walk toward the library. Obviously I need to clear the air, but I'm too focused on the case. I just need to see some of the papers from back then and see what they say. I'll talk to her properly afterwards.

The State Library is a big, imposing old building with Roman columns and a wide forecourt of grass where loads of people are sitting in the sunshine. There's also a big chess board painted on the ground to one side of the building, scattered with giant chess pieces almost the size of chairs. A few old guys are sitting round, smoking and watching a couple of nerdy looking guys play this nutty, supersized game.

In the foyer we sort out a locker for our stuff, and head to the archives section. We spend the next hour looking through the library catalogues, only speaking if we find something. We uncover some old editions of the *Bellanta Courier* using a microfilm reader. Such weird, ancient tech! I've seen most of the articles before, but one gives us some new info.

*Robin James Winter has been missing for three months. On 1 March 2010 Robin disappeared from his home at 18 Mather Street, Bellanta. Robin was last seen by his mother, Jane Winter, around 2 pm. She reported him missing around 5 pm that day after an extensive search around the house and neighbourhood.*

*Over fifty police officers and local volunteers, led by Detective Frank Firelli, have spent weeks searching the local area. A specialist police squad, known as Taskforce Torana, was sent to Bellanta from Sydney to assist the investigation in mid-March. The police searched every house in the local area several times. Further investigation, including a search of a nearby creek by a dive team and forensic testing, failed to reveal any clues about his disappearance. An information van was situated at the end of Mather Street two days after his disappearance. A local psychic even contacted the police, offering her help. But the police are no closer to recovering Robin.*

*An anonymous report made to police suggested that Robin may have been abused or neglected by his mother, who was suspected of dealing drugs. Jane Winter's ex-boyfriend Mark Reynolds was initially interviewed, but he was released without charge. Although several other people were questioned in connection to the case, no arrests have been made.*

An abused or neglected child? A drug-dealing mother?

'Oh shit!' Shell whistles. I stare at the screen, mouth open. This is too much.

I bolt out of the library, stumbling through all the people on the steps outside, gasping for air. I don't know what to do. I can't face going underground to catch the train home so I just stand there on the lawn, in limbo.

Shell comes after me, with our bags from the locker. 'Gus, are you okay?'

I shake my head, my stomach somersaulting.

I thought this would open up the investigation, but now it's all blurry, like I'm looking down the wrong end of a telescope.

She takes my hand and I try to slow my breathing. It's getting harder and harder to fight the fishhooks.

# Chapter 13

# Letter

Thursday finally arrives. I was up half the night, thinking about that article and searching for more information. Detective Frank Firelli would be the best person to talk to. If I went to the police about this, I wonder if they would let me contact him? I bet he'd know stuff that's off the record. I've watched enough crime shows to know that old cops often seem to know who really did it, even if they don't have enough evidence to charge them.

I'm antsy at school all day. Everyone's talking about this ridiculous Business Studies assignment, but what possible use is this to me right now?

Shell and I meet at lunchtime. She isn't wearing make-up today, which is rare. Her eyes look so much smaller without all the black eyeliner. I guess she is moving toward her more authentic look.

'I've been thinking about doing some kind of eco-business for that assignment. Like maybe a bike repair pop-up, to stop people just buying new bikes all the time?'

I grunt, distracted.

'What are you going to do?'

I look up. 'Dunno. I don't care about school at all right now.'

Shell catches her breath. 'Oh. Today's the day you get the DNA results, yeah?'

'Yep, hopefully.'

'I hope the results will give you some kind of answer, one way or another.'

I nod and take a breath.

She reaches out to touch my arm. 'Hey, that article we found. How much is it worrying you?

Another grunt. I can barely meet her eyes.

'It's not *definitely* true that she abused Robin or that she was a drug dealer. You only have surface information, nothing concrete.'

'True, but it's hard to get out of my head.'

She nods.

'I'll text you tonight if the DNA test turns up,' I say, getting up to leave.

'Sure. Are you okay?'

'Yes. We need to talk about you next.' I try to smile.

She gives me a tired nod.

* * *

I just get home from school and haven't even put my bag down when I get a text from Kane.

IT'S HERE.

I text him I'm on my way and head back out the door.

'Where are you going?' Mum calls as I go.

'Just have to see Kane about something,' I yell over my shoulder. When I get to the granny flat the door's locked. I knock furiously.

'It's me.'

'What's the password?' Kane says in a stupid voice from the other side of the door.

'What? Let me in.'

'What's the password?'

Jesus, what a time to try and be funny. 'Open up, you dick!'

'Close enough.' He opens the door holding the envelope behind his back, grinning like Carlton's won the grand final. 'Ta-dah!'

'Give it to me.'

'Bet you say that to all the boys!'

Coming out to Kane was easy. Having to listen to his lame gay jokes, less so.

I snatch it from him. It's a plain envelope, no branding to keep the contents discreet, I guess. I turn it around in my hands, back and forth.

I sit down on his sofa. 'Now I have it, I don't want to open it.'

'Why not? You've come this far.'

'Because . . .'

'Because you're scared of what it might say?'

'More like scared of what it doesn't say.'

Kane's confused. 'Eh?'

It's hard to explain. If these results show that Mum *isn't* my biological mother, then who is she? Whether I am Robin, or there's some other explanation, nothing will be the same again. And what does that mean about Dad? Was he not my real dad either?

My head swims.

Kane sits down next to me. 'Do you want me to open it for you, Goose?'

I shake my head. 'I'll do it. Just not right now. I need to take a run up at it, if that makes sense?'

'A hundred per cent. But don't leave it too long and get trapped in your head. Just rip it off, like a Bandaid.'

He knows me well.

I stand up and shove the letter in my back pocket.

Kane stands up too and pats my shoulder in a strangely reassuring way. 'Text when you've opened it. I'm meant to go to a footy club fundraiser tonight but I probably won't go,' he says as I leave.

'You still avoiding the club because of your knee?'

He looks sheepish. 'Not avoiding it, I just hate being on the sidelines.'

'Not being the hero of the club, the brilliant . . . um . . . striker?' I bait him.

'*Full forward*. It's not soccer!'

Got him. Still, I notice that he hasn't answered the question. Surely he's not serious about not knowing who he is without footy?

\* \* \*

At home, I decide to take Kane's advice and rip the Bandaid off. This might be the most important letter of my life. Or not. Either way, when I get back to my bedroom, I take it out of my pocket to read – then I put it away again. I'm not ready yet. If I'm honest, part of me ordered that test out of spite when I was angry with Mum.

I go out to the kitchen and rummage through the fridge for something to eat. Anything. There's a small container of leftover pasta that I zap in the microwave, drown in cheese, and shovel into my mouth. When I feel wound up like this I can eat faster than the speed of light.

Suddenly I realise Mum is watching me from the lounge room. 'I can make you something if you want?'

I shake my head, go back to my room and grab the envelope, and walk out to the front yard.

Why does the house look different tonight? The red roof seems less brightly coloured than usual. The weatherboards seem greyer, and even the verandah seems insubstantial. It's like someone has turned down the colour setting on the TV.

I rip open the letter and skim through the boring bits talking about the sample method and statistics around genetic markers blah blah blah until I get to the results section.

> 'Based on our analysis and the biostatistical evaluation of the results, it is practically proven, with a 91% probability, that Sample A is not a biological relation of Sample B.'

My head is on fire, my thoughts racing in every direction. If she's not my biological mother, who is she? Why am I living with her? Did she take me? Did Dad?

I take a picture of the letter to share with Shell and Kane later.

The house looms over me. It doesn't look like home. It's more like a haunted house now, and I might be the biggest ghost of all.

# Chapter 14

# Lighter

Back inside, Mum is sitting at the kitchen island, glass of wine in one hand, magazine in the other, a smoke burning in the ashtray in front of her. She's picking at some water crackers and a small tin of tuna. Not enough to feed a bird.

I take a breath and jump right in. 'I have something to show you.' I try to meet her eyes as best I can.

'What?'

I hand her the DNA results.

She barely even looks at the letter. 'What's this when it's at home?'

'We had to do DNA testing for that school assignment I told you about.' I lie.

'What? I thought you needed a birth certificate? You didn't tell me about this.' She's glaring at me. 'It's unethical for the school to have anything to do with DNA testing, let alone without parental consent,' she says, picking up the letter and reading intently.

I show her the results section on the page. 'This is the interesting part. It says that you and I' – I gulp, stalling – 'are not biologically related.'

I step back to watch her reaction.

'What?' Her voice is oddly high. She takes a slow drag on her smoke, her hand shaking.

'Read it. It says we don't share enough genetic material to

be considered related. There's a 91% chance that you're not my biological mother.'

She stares at me in shock. 'That's ridiculous!' Her voice is still strange and high-pitched. 'No. These results can't be right. I've never had a DNA sample taken.'

Shit. I have to tell her. I look down at my feet. 'I . . . um, I took some hairs from your hairbrush and had them tested against mine. These are the results. We're not related.'

She stands up and grabs me by the chin, pulling my face really close to hers. 'You stole from me to do some dodgy test for a, frankly, unethical *school assignment*? I'll be complaining to the principal about this.'

I back away a little, escaping her grip. 'The *point* is that you and I are not related.'

'Rubbish,' she says, 'the test is wrong. I bet the hairs weren't mine.'

'Who else would be using your brush?'

'I don't know! It's just a mistake. Maybe it's because of the medication I'm on?'

*Shit.* Could her medication really affect the testing somehow? That never crossed my mind.

She gets up in my face again and stares at me intensely. 'Why would you do this to me? All I have ever done is love you and protect you. And in return you throw this at me!'

I feel like I can't breathe, but I have to keep going now.

'I need to know where I came from. Why won't you show me my birth certificate? Why won't you talk about these results?'

She looks away and sits back down, rubbing her eyes. She picks up her smoke and rolls it around in her fingers. 'I've never shown you your birth certificate because it's *modified*.'

I frown, holding my hands up in confusion. 'What? What's that even mean?'

'It's what they give you when you adopt a child. Because you were *adopted*, not abducted.'

'What?'

'You heard me. Adopted. You were adopted when you were a toddler.'

I can't believe what she is saying. I literally cannot breathe. I put my head in my hands and take deep breaths, but the fishhooks are too strong. How can she have kept this from me?

'And you're just telling me this now? Why have you never said anything?'

She shakes her head and takes a deep drag on her smoke. 'We intended to tell you one day, but does knowing improve your life? We wanted you when someone else didn't. That's all you need to know. I'm your mother, whether you like it or not.'

I'm feeling panicky and faint-headed, like I'm going to fall over. I steady myself against the kitchen island. I can't believe I'm adopted. It would explain so much ... but for some reason I don't quite believe her. She's upset and she's angry, but there's something else in her face I can't read. She's had years to tell me this and hasn't. Only now, when I bring up this kidnap story, does she come out with this. In among all the swirling in my head, I can't help wondering if this isn't the whole story. I take a deep breath.

'Okay, where was I adopted from? Who were my birth parents?'

She stands up again, her hand clawing at the DNA letter on the table. 'Stop, Angus! You accuse me of everything under the sun, but then don't listen to my answers. And now you suddenly want to ask a hundred more questions. I understand that this is a shock, but I know nothing. Some birth parents choose to remain anonymous.'

'You must know *something*?'

She pushes past me. 'I'm really hurt by this, Angus. You have no idea what you've done, digging all of this up!'

I feel sick now, deep in my guts, but I have to get answers.

'Why can't you answer me?'

She whirls around to face me, furious. 'Get out!' she screams. 'Get out of here now!'

I open my mouth to speak again, but there's no point. I turn and go out into the backyard. She slams the door behind me.

I watch her through the kitchen window. Mum holds the DNA letter over the sink and sets it on fire with her lighter. It starts to smoulder and burn. Her crazed, sad eyes are lit up by the flames till she drops it in the sink.

Suddenly, she lets out a primal scream like an animal that has been kicked, and breaks down in tears. She sees me watching and moves away from the window.

It feels like the curtain between me and the world is burning away too now. Alone in the dark yard, I start to bawl too, crying like a little kid.

The dark shape of the cubbyhouse calls me. I wonder if Robin has been hidden somewhere inside of me all these years?

## Chapter 15

# Confetti

My head is spinning and I can't work out where I am. I try to blink but behind my eyelids is an explosion of colour, like someone has thrown confetti under them.

I wake up to see Kane leaning over me, calling out my name. His expression is dark, like he has bad news. I don't understand why I seem to be lying on the floor.

I sit up a bit but sink back down again, too lightheaded to stay up. 'Steady,' says Kane. His hand supports my head like I'm a baby.

I open my eyes properly. Kane's staring at me, looking angry but worried.

I'm on his bathroom floor. There's a bottle of whiskey on the floor beside me, half-empty. And Dad's Swiss Army knife is by my right hand.

No detective work required here.

Memories come flooding back. After Mum burned the DNA results, my feelings were shooting out in every direction. I needed to contain them, redirect them somehow. I went to the cubbyhouse and grabbed the knife out of its little wooden box. I heard Mum open the back door, so I crouched down low, out of sight. She stood on the back steps and called out to me. 'Gus? I'm sorry. Where are you?' I didn't respond. As she walked around the far side of the house, I crept back out of the cubbyhouse and ran down the driveway. I couldn't cut there; she'd find me.

I snuck over to Kane's place, not sure if he'd be home or not. When I knocked on the door there was no answer, so I grabbed the emergency key from round the back, and let myself in, shutting the door behind me. Flicking the light on, I flopped on his bed, fiddling with the knife. I tried to do what Dr Yamada taught me, taking in air in long, deep breaths. In. Out. In. Out.

That's when I spotted the bottle of whiskey on the kitchen bench. I grabbed it and took a swig. It tasted rough, but I took another swig, then another, enjoying the burning sensation as it went down. This was a better way to block things out.

That's all I remember. I guess I must have fallen asleep.

I can't meet his eyes. 'Sorry,' I mutter.

He pulls me up into a sitting position and leans me against the bathroom cabinet. The door handle sticks into my back but I'm feeling too groggy to move. 'Let's sober you up, you dick.' He wets a face washer with some cold water and rubs it on my face.

I can hear my phone buzzing.

'It's your mum,' says Kane. 'She's been ringing you non-stop. And she knocked on the door but I said you weren't here.'

'We had a fight.' I tell him about confronting Mum with the DNA results, and her burning the letter. 'She told me I'm adopted.'

'What?'

'Yeah, like that's the big secret. But I don't believe her.'

'Okay, let's talk about that later. You were passed out in my house with a knife. I thought you'd killed yourself or something for a minute! Scared the shit out of me. You can't keep avoiding what's going on Goose. You have to do something about it.'

It must have been awful for him. 'I'm sorry.' I mumble, knowing how weak it sounds.

'There has to be another way to manage it.'

A rush of tenderness and gratitude floods over me. How cool is he to do this for me? Kane is the best friend ever. I lean in and try to kiss him.

He backs away quickly. 'Whoa, back off mate!'

I am horrified. I just want the roof to fall in and crush me. Why did I do that? What is wrong with me?

'I'm sorry. I'm drunk and—' I didn't know what else to say. I want to throw up.

'I should call your mum.'

'No, please!'

'You make it really hard to help you sometimes.'

I stand up slowly, avoiding both the mirror and his eye as best I can. I do need to throw up. Quickly, I turn my head to the toilet, just in time to puke on target. There's so much of it, rushing out of me so fast it burns my throat.

'Ergh, gross.' Kane hands me a towel. It has a Dalek from *Doctor Who* on it. Of course it does. Shamefully I wipe my mouth, then squirt some toothpaste on my finger and run it over my gums. I am such a loser.

'Finished? Go lay on the bed if you're not gonna puke again. I'll make some coffee,' he says.

Obediently I lie back on Kane's bed, eyes closed, head spinning. I drift off to sleep, waking to the sound of Kane and Shell talking in the kitchen. Shell's head is almost shaved bald now.

Kane is whispering to Shell. 'He needs to talk to his mum again. And if she doesn't have the answers he wants, then I'll take him to the cops. He needs to sort this shit out now.'

Shell tilts her head to the side. 'I agree, but he has to do it when it's right for him. You can't force him into it.'

Kane rolls his eyes. 'Whatever, have it your way. But we need to do something.'

They look over, catching me watching. Kane eyes me warily. 'Awake now, are we?' he mutters.

Shell comes over to the bed and kicks one of its legs. 'Wiping yourself out isn't the answer, you know.'

'Yeah, listen to her,' Kane says.

I'm not ready to talk about it yet. 'What's with your hair?' I ask.

'The skinhead look is in.' Kane smirks.

'Shut up meathead. It's just something I wanted to try.'

'It is *very* short,' I say.

'I told you I was going to cut my hair. Don't you like it?'

'Yeah, but I thought you were just going shorter, not shaving it all off!'

'Whatever, I like it. We need to talk about . . . whatever's going on here.'

Kane nods. 'You're all over the joint Gus.'

Shell points to the whiskey bottle on the bathroom floor. 'And your coping mechanisms are totally sketchy. Still, I guess it's better than cutting yourself up in that shitty cubbyhouse.'

'We oughta knock that down,' adds Kane.

I feel ashamed and weird now that they are both calling me out so openly. My throat is dry and my eyes are stinging. I know they're both right. I just have to find the courage to do something. 'I need to get some answers. That's what I need.' I grab my phone to see where the nearest police station is.

Shell puts her hand on my arm. 'Wait, before you do anything, tell us what brought on this binge session.'

I have to tell them the whole story, in detail.

'I showed Mum the DNA results and she said I was adopted. But she wouldn't tell me anything else. Then she burned the letter and kicked me out.'

'What? So she really isn't your biological mother?' Shell says, wide-eyed.

'No. And remember how she was cagey about showing me my birth certificate? Something's not adding up.'

Shell lets out a long breath. 'Jeez Gus, that's a lot to take in at once. Being adopted answers some of your questions though, doesn't it?'

'I don't know why, but no. It feels like she's trying to distract me from the truth. I wish Dad was alive, he'd know what to do.'

'Aren't there agencies that help you find your real parents? Or, like, databases you can look at?' asks Kane.

I shake my head. 'There are, but the problem is that I don't even know if Angus is my real name, or if Cooper is Mum's real maiden name. I don't know anything!'

Shell looks worried. 'This is huge, Gus, but I think you need to give your mum a chance to explain. It's a lot for her too.'

I nod and lie back down, exhausted. Fighting with Mum, getting drunk, wanting to cut, trying to kiss Kane . . . I am such a mess.

* * *

When I wake up again the next morning, I know what I need to do. I tell Kane and Shell that I want to go to the police.

'I thought we agreed that you should talk to your mum one more time, before doing this?' says Shell. Kane nods his agreement.

Kane and Shell may be on the same page, but I *know* Mum is lying to me. Or at least covering something up. Maybe it's to do with Robin, maybe not. But how can she dismiss the aged-up picture on that website? This is actually happening to me. It's not just in my head.

'She's lying, Shell. I think I need some evidence about the case before I talk to her again. Something real.'

She nods. 'Okay, but first you need to clean up. You smell gross.'

'More like rank,' Kane says.

They're right. I stink. I need to go home to shower and change.

'Want me to come?' Shell asks.

'Nup. I got this.' I should probably say yes, but I feel I really do need to do this on my own.

'You sure you're okay?'

'I'm sure.'

I sneak in through the back door. It's still early, so I figure Mum's still in bed. I head into my room and chuck my stained shirt on the floor. I'll have to make do with a deodorant shower. A real one will wake her up. I pull on a navy blue shirt. It isn't 'Salute Blue', the colour of Victoria Police uniforms, but I feel like navy is the right colour to wear somehow. I grab a backpack and chuck some socks and undies and clothes in there, as well as my laptop, charging cords, some toiletries, my anti-depressants and my wallet. I dig out $122 in cash I have in my drawer and stuff it in my wallet.

I make sure I still have the photo I took of the DNA letter, then I step quietly into the hall.

Mum comes out of the bathroom just as I'm sneaking past her door. She actually screams a little when she sees me, making us both jump.

'Where were you last night? I was worried.' She looks exhausted, dark bags under her eyes, hair all over the place. She's still in her dressing gown and I can see scratch marks on her legs.

'You chucked me out, remember?'

'I didn't mean for you to stay out all night. I just wanted you to get out of my face.' Her face softens. 'Sorry Angus. I was shocked and, frankly, angry.'

'Are you going to answer any of my questions?'

'Look, it's complicated. Come into the kitchen and—'

'So you can set something else on fire? No thanks.'

'Angus, we *have* to talk.'

I'm the angry one now. 'I've been trying to talk to you for days. It's too late now. I'm staying at Kane's.'

She looks shaky as she eyes my bulging backpack. 'For how long?'

'Until I can get my head together.'

Tears start spilling down her cheeks. 'Don't go like this.' She puts her arm out in front of me to stop me leaving. I push past.

'Angus, please!'

'Call me when you're ready to tell me the real truth,' I snap as I leave.

\* \* \*

I bolt back over to Kane's, feeling like I'm on the edge of a panic attack.

He and Shell are gone, so I chuck my bag on the bed and go and lay on the bathroom floor and close my eyes. Cold tiles help bring me out of a panic attack. Dr Yamada taught me that. *Soak up the cold*, he says. After a while on the floor I feel my heart start to slow again. I open my eyes and spot a small pool of spilled whiskey on the floor.

Time to get some real answers.

## Chapter 16

# Police

Even though I had wanted to be a cop forever, I never really met a real one until the night of the accident, when an officer helped me out of our wrecked car. A strong figure, looking down at me and telling me that everything would be okay. With chaos swirling around me, I believed him.

Mum and Dad had taken me out with them to some big industry dinner for Dad's work. The drive there was tense. They had been arguing for the last couple of days since the tunnel incident.

The dinner was at this fancy restaurant in Hawthorn. Mum had to explain what all the different knives and forks were for. The room was huge, dotted with tables covered in white tablecloths and elaborate centrepieces. There were also several bottles of wine on each table, which Mum was making the most of.

Dad drove because he wanted to stay sober among all of the senior management types, but he didn't really drink that much anyway. He spent quite a bit of time talking to people at different tables, leaving me and Mum on our own. He was talking in particular to Mr Carlson, his boss, a big, bloated, red-faced guy who seemed to fill up the room with his booming voice.

During the night Mum spilled a glass full of wine over herself in front of Dad's colleagues and jokingly blamed him. He was not happy. They had some quiet words at the table, and she told him to lighten up through gritted teeth. Dad took her out into the foyer and they argued some more as I watched from our table. Mum was fuming when she came back, saying something about going home early. She grabbed my hand and walked me out of the venue to the car. Dad must have realised what was happening not long after we left. He came running over to the car just as Mum was starting the ignition. He told her to get in the passenger seat and that he'd drive us home.

I don't remember what happened next really, but I kinda pieced it together from things Mum said and what the police told me later. A few blocks from home a dog came bounding out onto the road. It seems that when Dad swerved to miss it, the car ran up the gutter and rammed hard into a tree, destroying the bonnet diagonally. The impact broke a huge tree branch, which came in through the top of the windscreen on Dad's side, and down into the footwell on Mum's side. Dad suffered a huge blow to the head, and the branch mangled Mum's legs. They were showered with glass and there was a lot of blood. I was in the back seat, behind Dad, but I didn't really get hurt at all, just thrown about.

While I don't remember much of the accident myself, I do remember that sound of the tree crushing into the car. It was like a gate howling open in hell.

It was only later at hospital that we found out Dad had an intercranial brain bleed. They had to put him into a medical coma to reduce the pressure on his brain.

*  *  *

The local police station is a bland grey concrete building, a combined station and lock-up. I hoped that by the time I got here I would have a better idea of what exactly I was going to say. I had hoped to feel strong or competent or at least one of the two. But no. I'm shit-scared, and still feeling sick from the whiskey.

I bite the bullet and walk through the door, a *whoosh* of cold air blowing around me. There is a wide desk in the foyer with the Victoria Police logo emblazoned on it. Behind the desk is a constable in uniform. He's in his early twenties, tanned, handsome – he belongs on a recruitment poster.

I step up to the desk and just start talking. 'Hi. This is a bit random but I want to find out some information about a kidnap case from thirteen years ago.'

The constable doesn't bat an eyelid. Presumably working the front desk you hear and see it all. 'What exactly do you want to know – and why?' he responds indifferently.

'Well, I found this case on an unsolved crime website,' I take my laptop out of my backpack and open it to show him the website with Robin's picture, 'and they do this thing where they age up photos of kids who were kidnapped years ago.'

The constable stares at me. 'And?'

'Uh . . . well, there was this photo that came up and it looks just like me.'

He looks at the screen more closely, then at me (I blush), then back at the picture. His left eyebrow rises a bit.

I didn't think this through. What do I say now? 'I think it might have been me who was kidnapped all those years ago.'

His eyebrow goes up higher still, like in a cartoon. He says nothing for like a full minute. Finally he speaks. 'What's your name?'

'Angus Green.'

'Okay, let me get the duty supervisor to talk to you.'

I expected to be dismissed or laughed at, so this is a surprise. I sit down on one of the chairs along the far wall and pick up one of the VicPol newsletters sitting there, flicking through it while the constable is on the phone. I can't quite make out what he is saying, despite straining my ears. Maybe I need to learn how to lip-read as part of my preparation for joining the force.

The constable calls out from behind the desk and says that someone will be out to see me shortly. I nod stupidly, sitting there swinging my legs back and forth like a little kid.

This is an unreal moment. For all I know I might go in there and my life might change forever.

I scan the posters on the wall. 'Stay under .05', 'Report domestic violence', 'Rape alert', 'Dob in a dealer'. No posters about cold cases.

'Angus Green?' says a voice nearby. I look round and see a friendly-looking woman in her late twenties with super curly brown hair, dressed in a sergeant's uniform. She's holding out her hand to me.

I nod and shake her hand.

'I'm Sergeant East. Let's have a little chat, shall we?'

She gestures toward the set of double doors she came through. Together we walk into an open-plan office with various officers sitting at desks. No one looks up as I come in. I want to soak it all in, my first time behind the scenes at a cop shop, but she quickly guides me into an interview room. Not a dark, enclosed room like I've seen on TV, but an open glassed room with a table and chairs, and a water cooler. There's a big box of tissues on the table. Ominous.

We sit down opposite each other. In front of her is a desktop computer that she starts typing on as I speak. 'Alright then. Constable McSween on the front desk told me what you told him. How about you tell me everything, starting at the beginning please? I'm going to start what we call an information report, or IR. This will then go into our computer system.'

I stare at my hands, embarrassed. 'I've always been interested in old unsolved crimes. I read a lot about them on the internet ...

I mean loads, seriously. The other day I found this missing kid website . . .'

Ten minutes later, I have garbled out my story. Not just the facts and the test results, but some of my general crap about Mum as well. I bet she's bored. She's probably typing her grocery list.

'And then I spoke to Mum but of course she denied the whole thing. She says that she and Dad adopted me. I want to believe her. But what if it's not true? This DNA test shows that we're not related. That may mean nothing, but why wouldn't they have told me earlier? And why deny the photo even looks like me when it clearly does? What if I really am Robin Winter?' I stop, breathless.

'That's quite a story,' Sergeant East says as she finishes typing.

I can tell by her face that she doesn't believe me. Her eyes are fixed on me, but it's like they are looking somewhere else at the same time.

I look her straight in the eye for the first time. 'I need to know the truth.'

Sergeant East smiles at me like I'm a kid having a tantrum. 'Try not to let your imagination run too wild just yet. We have to stick to the facts, and there aren't many. This is just the beginning.'

I nod, feeling fairly patronised at this point. 'So what happens now?'

'I'll pass this information on to the detectives in our Intel unit. They will likely contact NSW colleagues, as this case was in their jurisdiction. A missing person is not cleared off our system until they have been located, so something will be there still. Then someone will likely contact you.'

She can see I was hoping for more. 'Look, for all we know the ad is a fake. Anyone may be able to upload cases to the site, especially if it's free, for whatever reason they want. Some of these sites attract weirdos. The whole entry could be a hoax of some kind.'

I never thought of that. I can feel sweat dripping down my forehead.

'I looked up the case in the old Bellanta papers. The main suspect was Jane Winter's ex, Mark Reynolds, but there were several other suspects. Lots of articles mention Detective Frank Firelli, the original lead detective. Could I talk to him, given he led the case right from the start?'

Sergeant East shakes her head. 'You cannot contact Detective Firelli or any other officer involved in the case. This is a police matter and you're a minor. Leave this to us. We must follow procedure.'

I figured she'd say that.

'Do you believe me?' I ask.

She seems a little surprised by the question. 'Well, your story is based on almost no evidence, but I'll pass it onto our intel unit and see what they think.'

*What, that's it?* I hoped they'd be able to bring up some information on the computer system that they could share with me. 'Can't you look up the case now and see what's there? DNA samples or witness statements maybe? I need to know.'

'No, I can't share that information,' she says, firmly. 'Calm down and leave it with me.'

Sergeant East leads me back to the front counter. The constable is trying to appease an old drunk lady who is slurring out accusations. She seems to be saying someone has stolen her crocodile.

What a waste of time that was. Even if the case is in a different state, surely all their records are linked? And why can't I talk to the original investigating detective? She totally thinks I'm a fraud.

The more I think about it, the more I realise that I need to go to Bellanta. I'm tinkering around the edges here – it's time to go to the source and dig up the truth.

## Chapter 17

# Cheezels

I head back to Kane's place, making sure Mum isn't watching out the window. I'm surprised to see Shell there again. They both look awkward in each other's company, though they seem to be sharing a box of Cheezels. She jumps up as I come in the door. 'How'd you go?'

I tell them about what happened at the police station.

Shell is angry on my behalf. 'You're offering them clues to an unsolved case. I don't get why they aren't more interested. I'd have a cop car over at your place by now, interviewing your mum.'

'Could the DNA test be wrong?' Kane pipes up.

'Dunno. Anyway, the sergeant said they need real evidence and it seems the DNA test isn't enough, since it just proves I'm not biologically related to Mum, nothing else. Anyway, she said she'd look into it. But I don't know if she will or if she was just saying what I wanted to hear to get rid of me. I'm pretty sure she thought I was a liar.'

Shell shakes her head. 'She won't have thought that because you aren't.'

She can tell I'm not convinced, so she puts a Cheezel on each finger and comes at me, hands like a tiger's claws. Kane chucks one in the air and catches it in his mouth. Suddenly they're like a circus act.

Kane, chewing noisily, says, 'You know what you need to do now, don't you?'

I smile. I know what he's going to say. 'I need to go to Bellanta.

Visit the scene of the crime. See if I can find out what happened to Jane and Mark and Robin. Suss out Firelli, if he's still there. Talk to people. Look up the paper archives.'

'You're not going without me,' Shell says.

'I have just the fine vehicle to get us there,' says Kane. Shell and I both roll our eyes, smiling.

'Road trip!' laughs Shell, clapping her hands. Cheezels go everywhere.

'It's a long weekend, so no school for you two and I can change my shifts. Let's tell everyone we're going to Lake Kalona camping or something, but head up north instead,' Kane says.

'It's only like four hours away,' I say.

Shell snickers. 'My parents will never believe I'm going camping.'

My phone rings. Mum again. She keeps calling, even though I haven't picked up any of her calls. I'm glad that she cares but I'm also still angry with her. I need to find out a bit more before I can talk to her properly.

I feel like I will get the answers I need in Bellanta. Maybe Jane Winter is still there? Or Mark Reynolds? Or the real kidnapper? Or the person from the website who is looking for Robin?

The road trip is on.

\* \* \*

That night, lying on Kane's sofa, I can't get to sleep. I text Shell and get a response pretty quick.

*I'm worried about going to Bellanta.*

*It'll be fine. You'll find that cop, and all the answers that you need.*

She's right, provided Frank Firelli is still even there. They say cops never forget their unsolved cases. I hope that's true.

I keep thinking about this trip Mum, Dad and I took to Lake Kalona years ago for Dad's work. Mr Carlson was a boating fanatic and had organised a family event at the lake.

'Can I go on Mr Carlson's boat this year?'

Mum turned to me, laughing. 'Maybe. Mind you, I wouldn't trust him driving a toy car, let alone a boat.'

I nodded and went to my room, returning minutes later with my old blow-up floaty around my waist. It was green, with a frog's head at the front. I loved it.

Mum burst out laughing when she saw me in it, the frog head squished out of shape as I was far too big for it, even then. She prodded the plastic. 'Still works, I see.'

So, off we went, via the nearby servo. Dad filled up the tank and went in to pay, returning with an ice cream for me. Mum glared at him. 'Why are you filling him up with junk?' He looked away, not responding.

Eventually we arrived and parked in a clearing on the side of the lake, near all the other cars. The lake stretched out before us, blue and wide and very impressive. The sun was high and twinkling on the water, like a painting. There were several boats on the water already, looking cool and sleek. Further along, near a bend in the lake, I could see the end of a jetty where various houseboats were moored. I liked the idea of living alone on a houseboat, drifting with the tide, and taking off to a new place whenever you felt like it.

Dad had bought this elaborate umbrella and fancy tarp, making it more like setting up camp than having a spot of lunch and some fun in the water on a hot Sunday. There were quite a few people set up with multiple eskies, radios blaring, chairs reclined. Lots of wine and beer flowing already. And here was my dad with all this gear and no idea how to set it up, a sitcom cliché.

Mum let me explore, saying something about not wandering too far. I actually walked just a little way ahead and hid behind a tree so I could spy on them, like a good investigator. I could hear Mum talking. 'Please stop buying him junk food, he's getting fat.'

'I'm not,' I cried out from behind the gum tree. Dad made this deflating noise, while Mum jumped up with her hand covering her mouth as if to push the words back in.

I remember starting to cry and then, for whatever reason, wet my pants.

Nearby some of Dad's workmate's kids had turned to see what was going on and saw my wet pants. One of them started laughing and pointing at me, yelling 'Piss pants!'

Horrified, I ran off toward the public toilet block.

Inside, it stank of stale piss. There were cobwebs in the corners and dry gum leaves on the concrete floor.

Mum came bolting in. 'I'm sorry, Gussy.' She helped me take off my wet pants and rinsed them for me in the hand basin. Then she wrung the excess water out of them, and, holding them flat, put the pants under the hand dryer and started to dry them. When the cycle stopped, she would start the dryer again.

I watched her closely, grateful and relieved. She was resourceful, like a girl scout. 'There we go,' she said eventually, holding out the now-dry pants to me.

I put them on and looked up at her, smiling.

'Now you better go meet these other kids,' she said.

'They'll laugh at me,' I protested.

'No, they won't,' she said, and she was right. The other kids weren't mean at all. And the one who had laughed and pointed was sitting in the back seat of a car, punished by their parents, I guess.

Later in the afternoon Mr Carlson came over and immediately started telling us about his new speedboat, no hello or anything. It was a five-footer, fire-engine red, with *Carlson on the Sea* painted on the side. Big deal.

Mum was trying not to laugh as he donned a sea captain's hat and started working out who was coming in the boat for a ride first and who was going to ski or sit in the rubber tyre behind the boat. Mum kept me busy with something so we weren't first. I could see her eyes following the boat ripping across the lake, watching the skiers and the rubber donut bounce close to one another. But no one fell and no one got hit.

About the third time Mr Carlson came back to the shore and called out for volunteers, I put my hand up. I had pissed my pants in front of everyone, so I felt like I had something to prove.

'Are you sure Angus? It looks scary to me,' Mum said, giving me an out.

'Nonsense, let the boy have a go,' Mr Carlson said. Dad told me to go for it, probably for his boss' sake. She sighed in defeat, giving dad some serious side-eye, and returned to her wine.

The boat revved up and then took off with a twang, me sitting spread-eagled in the old tyre. Nothing happened for a moment, but then the tension on the rope hit and I was suddenly flying. I was shit-scared and exhilarated at the same time.

I was told later that a couple of people were even cheering me on from the shore, but all I could hear was the thrum of the engine and the roar of the water around me.

The boat came round for a turn, and I was pulled back and forth on the tyre, bouncing across the waves. Then there was another turn, and another. Each time it got bumpier but I held on tight. I would prove them all wrong.

Then Mr Carlson made a massive turn, and wave after wave hit me. I flew out of the tyre and into the water. I went under fast.

That's the last thing I remember till I was waking up back on land, with Mum crying over me, calling out my name. I had never seen her so upset.

It was alright though; I was just winded and a bit shocked. Mum gently wrapped me up in her big orange beach towel and her and Dad carrying me to the car. 'You never think of the bloody consequences of anything. *Ever*,' she hissed at Dad as we walked.

On the way home Mum got him to stop off and buy me another ice cream, which I loved. Two in one day!

We never really spoke about it again, but the next day she took me to the local pool. 'I'm going to teach you how to swim properly.'

# Chapter 18

# Bellanta

Big day, Saturday. Road trip day. If this was TV, it would be just chucking a couple of things in a bag and hotfooting it out of town. The other day when I grabbed some stuff from home I never really thought about going to Bellanta. I was just getting stuff for a night at Kane's. I really need more shirts and a clean pair of jeans, but I'm not risking going back to the house. I have enough doubts without Mum trying to talk me out of this.

I've had heaps of missed calls from her now. I texted her about the camping trip but didn't respond to her follow-up messages. She came to the front door asking to see me early this morning, while I was in the shower. I could hear Kane telling her that it was just a quick trip for the long weekend. She didn't sound happy.

Kane beeps the horn of the Kingswood and I jump in the front seat with him. When he first bought this car, I thought it was a bit of a joke, but now it seems like the best thing he ever did.

Fiona and Bob are standing on the verandah, waving us goodbye. Both in tracksuits and runners, of course.

I can see Mum watching from our front window, her outline a shadow behind the curtains, like a ghost. What is she thinking? Why is she just standing there, watching, doing nothing? Is she going to come out to stop me?

'Thanks for this,' I say. 'Can we get going?'

'It's cool. They bought the Lake Kalona camping story.'

Fiona comes up to the driver's window and hands him fifty bucks, giving him a concerned look. 'Make sure you don't run out of petrol, hon.' Unbelievable. Kane is totally lying to them about this trip, and now they're funding it!

Kane takes the money with a smile. My phone pings.

'Shell's texted, she's ready.'

Kane deftly manoeuvres the big car around a small roundabout as we head into Shell's street.

'Nice one, driver,' I say.

'Hey, Goose? I'm more than just the driver. I want to be a detective too.'

After the way he looked after me the other night, I owe this to him. 'You're definitely more than just the driver.'

'Cool.' He seems stoked.

'You're the muscle as well.' I laugh.

Shell's standing out the front of her house with a big black suitcase on wheels. She seems to have stopped wearing make-up altogether now, and she's wearing plain black jeans and a tight black Greenpeace T-shirt that shows off her boobs and belly. She usually wears big baggy stuff that covers her fat bits. We both do. Now it's all out there. I guess she's owning it more.

Her mother is standing in the doorway with a strained look on her face. I remember the conversation she had with me the other day. I wonder how much all these changes Shell is making is bothering her? I bet she's hating the lack of hair.

'What's all that for? We're going for one or two nights, max,' I say to Shell.

She grins. 'Cheryl thinks it's a very girly thing to do, to bring a huge suitcase for a couple of nights away. It's actually half empty.'

Kane gets out of the car to open the boot. He makes a move as if he's going to help her with the bag, but before he can, she lifts it up and into the boot in one swift motion.

She hops into the back seat and grins at both of us. 'Let's get this show on the road.'

Kane plugs 'Bellanta' into Google Maps on his phone, which is in the suction cup cradle he must have just bought. The car is so old, he has to use a cigarette lighter adapter with a USB slot to charge the phone and the speakers. Hilarious.

We drive around to a nearby servo and stock up on food and drinks for the trip. Kane gets a sports drink and a protein bar, while Shell and I get chips and soft drinks.

Then the biggest question of all: what do we listen to? The old Kingswood only has an AM radio, so the fight begins over whose Spotify playlist gets used. Kane has a lot of metal, which kinda drains you of life after a while. Shell's list is more indie, and mine is fairly gay pop.

Eventually we take off, with metal first ('It's my car,' says Kane). Up the Hume highway, toward the Murray River on the Victorian border. For the first time in ages my mind relaxes.

The first hours of the trip are uneventful. The trees and paddocks are full of rich colours. The vista stretches out endlessly, reminding me of how crowded living in the city can be. Here there is a real landscape, from the road to the horizon. With the windows down, cool breeze blowing in, loud music, and my friends by my side . . . this feels like a proper movie-style road trip.

As the drive goes by, we're listening to each other's music and gabbing away about all kinds of stuff. Kane seems a bit distracted, whereas Shell seems a bit more energetic than usual. Can a makeover (make *under*?) do that?

'I have some ideas about how we can divide up this job,' she says. 'Gus, you should go to the house first, see if it looks familiar, see what that tells you. Then, you and I should go to the newspaper to check their archives. Maybe we can go to the local hospital and see if they still have Robin's medical records? At the end of the day we can all meet up and go through everything we've found. Then go see if we can find Detective Firelli's place. How's that sound?'

'That makes sense,' I say.

'What about me, skinhead? What do I do?' asks Kane.

Shell shrugs. 'Drive, flirt with suspects . . .'

Kane snorts. He seems annoyed.

Shell turns to me, ignoring Kane. 'What are you going to say to the old detective if you find him?' Reasonable question.

'I have a list of things to ask on my phone, but they're random. They aren't a considered set of interrogation questions that will solve the case or stand up in court or anything. It's more just stuff that popped into my head in the middle of the night.' I turn my phone to Shell to show her the list.

- What do you think happened to Robin?
- Where is Jane Winter now? Did she keep looking for Robin?
- Who was Robin's father? Could he have taken Robin?
- What happened to Mark Reynolds?
- Who were the other suspects? Why were they never charged?

Shell hands me back my phone. 'Big questions.'

'It'd be good to find out more about the other suspects. None of the articles ever named them. I also want to know who was the last person to see Robin that day, how long the investigation went for, and why they gave up looking for him.'

'Remind me what we know about this Detective Firelli,' Shell says, ripping open a pack of chips with her teeth.

'He was the lead detective on the original case, but after a couple of weeks the Sydney police came to the town to take over the investigation. Seems he was taken off the case, I guess because he didn't solve it fast enough. He popped up in a random local paper article online that mentioned him buying a property out of town a few years back, so I have an address for him. I hope he's still there.'

I feel like a detective now, presenting in an incident room. I really need my timeline stretched out across those Perspex boards the cops use, armed with a Texta and pictures of Robin and the suspects.

But all I have is the pack of chips Shell just handed me.

'Basically, he's my best chance of finding out what's in the case report. And also what's not in it. Like, maybe they had no evidence for one of the suspects but they were still convinced that it was them.'

Shell smiles. 'They may know what happened to Robin but they just couldn't prove it?'

'That's what I'm hoping. Maybe after all this time he'll be willing to share.'

With that she settles back and we yak about other things. Kane is quiet, rubbing his knee occasionally. Maybe just concentrating on the drive. I wonder if he's in more pain than he lets on? I never thought I'd say this, but I miss his cocky swagger.

Three-and-a-half hours to Bellanta.

\* \* \*

As we cross into New South Wales, I realise I've never been interstate before. I've never really been anywhere before, now that I think about it.

Some of the towns we drive through are pretty big, others little more than a street. I like that they all seem to have big wide main streets, dotted with pubs, community gardens, souvenir shops, signs for farmer markets. There's lots of space in the country, a big contrast after the crowded side-by-side houses in Melbourne.

Along the roadside people are selling Granny Smith and Red Delicious apples, cow or chook shit for gardens, and even ugly sculptures made out of tyres and bicycle wheels. I spot a statue of a scary pig that looks like it would chew your face off.

We're about an hour out of Bellanta, but it's all getting a little real. Despite being so certain the picture on the website was me, I suppose a big part of me thought all this was just me and my friends investigating an old crime and having adventures along the way. But it's not like that anymore. I've unleashed this thing from the past and now I can't get it back in its box. I can't go back; I can only keep going. I don't know what I'm going to find here but it feels like the only way to get to the truth, and to stop this tornado turning round and round in my head.

'I googled it and the house was still there two years ago, but the pictures meant nothing to me,' I say, to break the silence in the car and my swirling thoughts.

'Mate, it could have changed a lot over the years,' Kane says quietly.

'You might get a flashback, like on every TV crime show ever,' Shell jokes.

I roll my eyes. 'Yep. That's what I'm aiming for, a black-and-white TV flashback as I stare into the distance.'

'Hey, imagine if you have a whole other birthday. How weird would that be?' says Kane.

'Of all the things that could impact him, *that's* what you think of?' snaps Shell.

There's silence for a minute as they glare at each other via the rear-view mirror. Kane cranks up the volume, blaring more metal out at us. Shell puts her headphones on to listen to something else.

Kane half-smiles at me from the corner of his mouth.

Soon we are on the outskirts of Bellanta, slowing down to sixty. I feel a panic rising up inside me. My heart is beating faster. I take some deep breaths and try to settle but it's not helping. I get Kane to pull over on the side of the road.

'You gonna puke?'

I shake my head, but I get out of the car and sit on the curb with my head between my knees, just in case.

'Don't think about the cubbyhouse, just breathe,' says Shell. Subtle as ever.

After a minute or so the feeling passes and I stand up.

'Want some lunch to settle your stomach?' Shell asks, pointing to the golden arches of a McDonald's up the road.

Great idea. Junk food and distraction. That's what I need. I plop back into the car and we drive down the road to the Macca's carpark, right over the road from a crappy-looking motel. Within five minutes I am jamming a Big Mac into my mouth like my life depends on it. Shell spots Kane looking at the motel.

'No way are we staying at that shithole.'

* * *

After everyone's finished eating, we pile back into the car and drive through the centre of town. There are some cars around, but it seems to be a quiet Saturday. There's the usual kind of shops along the street: bakery, souvenirs, cafe, two-dollar shop, and a big pub called the Union Club on the corner. It's just another town. Some shops look old and faded enough to have been here thirteen years ago. Nothing looks familiar; nothing sparks any memories.

We drive around a huge water fountain decorated with horses dramatically rearing up to the sky. Behind it sits an impressive old town hall building with this massive clock tower. It strikes midday as we drive past and, with our windows down, the weirdly distinctive, super loud chime echoes through the car like a foghorn.

We drive past a sign pointing to the Bellanta Base Hospital. Was Robin born there? A couple of minutes later, Kane turns toward Mather Street. We cross over a very murky-looking creek to get there. It's wide and looks deep. This must be the creek they mentioned in one of the articles. I shiver, imagining divers in wetsuits trawling the creek bed for Robin's body.

Mather Street is short, only about twenty houses by the looks, but wide, with tall plane trees lining the footpaths. The houses all have large front gardens. You don't see that much in inner Melbourne. There are one or two newer places, sitting next to mainly older, rundown homes. This was clearly a poor part of town. I spot number eighteen about halfway down the street, a small house with a FOR RENT sign out the front. Its pale yellow weatherboards and peeling brown front door really need a paint. The old iron roof looks original, and there's a small verandah that leads down to a dry lawn that's gone to seed. It looks abandoned.

I'm starting to feel overwhelmed again. 'Actually, why don't we do all of this together? If one of us turns up something I want us all to be there, if that's okay?'

Kane and Shell agree.

The three off us get out of the car and stand on the footpath outside the house. It's definitely the right place, but I check the address again, and a photo from the *Bellanta Courier* that showed the house back then. I stand there, staring, waiting for a memory to come flooding back.

'Anything?' asks Shell.

I shake my head. Nothing seems familiar, nothing at all. Not Bellanta. Not this street. Not even the house. Has this all been a waste of time?

At the front of the yard is a low brick fence. I walk over and sit on it, facing the street. Instinctively I want to swing my legs back and forth. It's far too low, but maybe it wouldn't be if I was two or three?

Did I play here? Did I see people coming and going? Did someone see me here alone that day?

There's a letterbox to my right. It's cobalt blue and shaped a bit like a triangle. The paint is old and chipped, so it could be from back when Jane and Robin were here. I don't remember it. I know they talk about people blanking out bad memories to protect themselves psychologically, but I'd have to remember *something*, even some random little detail, like a weird letterbox?

I get up and walk up the path to the front door. Maybe the current tenants are still here, despite the weathered FOR RENT sign. Or maybe a kidnap house stays empty, like a murder house, because people are superstitious. I'm too scared to knock on the door though, so I sneak a look around the back. On one side of the house is a tall trellis that once held vines or ivy maybe, but now it's just supporting dead twigs. The yard at the side is overgrown and has no distinctive features. Looks like there isn't really a backyard per se, just enough room for a washing line. The whole place feels like it's been empty for a long time.

Mum would freak out at the unmown lawn and the neglected garden. I wonder how she's going? I feel a pang of guilt for just taking off like this and not returning her calls or texts.

I wonder if the neighbours knew what was going on in this house. How can a little kid go missing in broad daylight without someone in the street seeing anything?

What do I do now? Do I go door to door and ask if anyone remembers a crime from years ago? I mean, this is a small-ish town, everyone would have known about it, right? It would have been a big deal, especially when the Sydney cops took over the investigation.

I wonder if anyone in the street is home in the middle of the day? I walk up and down the footpath, but none of the other houses on the street look familiar either.

That's when I notice that I'm being watched.

# Chapter 19

# Roses

Directly over the road is a cream-coloured weatherboard house that is old, but well maintained, with a neat front yard dotted with rose bushes. An elderly lady is watching me from a wicker chair on the verandah. Guess I look like someone casing the street to break into a house, or whatever old people think young people do these days.

Going to talk to her might stop her ringing the cops or neighbourhood watch or whatever, plus give me the chance to ask her some questions. I smile and wave to her. That confuses her a bit. She waves back tentatively.

I tell Kane and Shell I'm going to ask her some questions. As I walk up to her front fence, I google 'common types of roses' on my phone.

'Are these tea roses?' I ask her, leaning on the gate.

She eyes me hesitantly, like an old koala with a grey perm, a pink cardigan, a big cameo brooch, and thick round glasses. She is very frail looking, with dark eye bags and pale, papery skin.

'They are, dear, a hybrid orange tea rose, a varietal I breed myself.' She beckons me closer with a thin little hand.

I open the gate and walk up the rosebush-lined path. There's a large yellow rosebush in a pot by the door. The aroma of the flowers is strong, but nice, not cloying.

'Um . . . have you lived here long?'

'Oh yes, thirty-odd years or so,' she says.

'So you'd remember the Robin Winter case?'

This throws her. 'Yes.' She looks uncomfortable.

'I'm doing an assignment on the case for school and wanted to find out more about what happened. Not just what was in the papers, but what was it like for people in the street.'

'Well, I'm not sure . . .'

'Maybe we could just sit out here and talk, would that be okay? I'd like to hear your memories of that time.'

I can't believe I'm being so bold, but she seems okay with it. I wonder if people are just friendlier and more open to talking to strangers in the country? Maybe she's just lonely.

She studies me closely, probably trying to judge if I'm a serial killer or not. Her eyes are big and dark. I hope that means she's a keen observer, and that she watched what unfolded over the street all those years ago.

I sit in the wicker chair opposite her. I worry mine isn't strong enough to hold me, so I put my legs and feet out wide to support me in case it crumbles.

'My name is Angus Green.'

'I am Mrs Esther Crale. My husband Bill is just out the back, fixing the greenhouse doors. He used to be a carpenter, you see.'

I feel like she's making a point of him being close, so I know that she's not alone. Her hands are shaking. I hope that's because she's old, not because she's scared.

'So, you remember the Robin Winter case well?'

She smiles a little at me. 'Of course, it was all happening on my doorstep, dear. There were police blocking the roads and doing house-to-house searches. There were reporters out in the street every day. There was even a police caravan at the end of the street for a month where you could go and report any information you may have had.'

'It sounds bad.'

She smiles and shakes her head so much that the chain on her glasses jiggles on her chest. 'Oh no, it was thrilling! Just like a movie, dear.'

I can't figure out if this is funny or gruesome. Old people are weird.

'What was Jane Winter like? Do you remember when she first moved in here?'

Mrs Crale stares out across the street like she's looking back into the past.

'She was waifish but quite pretty, in a cheap kind of way. Ripped jeans, tight T-shirts that no lady would wear, especially when pregnant. She had lots of men interested in her.'

'Including Mark Reynolds?'

'Yes. He was a nice man. They courted for quite a while. He looked after her, and the boy as well. He was working at the local K-Mart store, a respectable lad.'

'"Courted"?'

'Mark and her were an item,' she winks.

'Ah, okay. What was he like?'

'Red hair, glasses, tall. Nice manners. They broke up when Robin was very young.'

'Do you know why?'

'I'm not one for gossip, dear,' she says, lowering her voice. 'But there were a lot of people coming and going at all hours, buying drugs from her, I gather. Mark wanted her to stop . . .' she pauses. 'Shouldn't you be writing this down?' She points at the still-closed notebook in my hand.

I forgot I'd said I was writing an assignment. I open up the notebook and start scribbling.

'So Jane and Mark broke up?'

'Yes. Later, she started courting a doctor, Ian Christow. He was an arrogant man, like most doctors. I was a nurse at a children's hospital for many years and have little time for doctors and their superior attitudes. I think they call it a god complex these days.' Her mouth puckers into what Mum calls a cat's bum.

'So you didn't like him as much as Mark?'

'Mark was kind and caring. But the doctor was pushy and controlling, and he and Jane argued a bit, from what I could see.'

Did she stand there at the window all day, watching them?

'Do you know who Robin's father was?'

She shakes her head and the chain on her glasses jiggles again. 'Nobody did.'

'That's alright. What was Robin like?'

She clasps her hands together, almost in prayer. 'He never had a chance. Mother selling drugs. All sorts of people coming in and out of the house. Poor thing used to sit in the dirt out in the front yard like an abandoned toy. He was a malnourished little mite.'

I feel my eyes start to sting.

'Do you remember the day he was taken?'

'Yes, I was gardening that afternoon.'

'Did you see anyone come to the house?'

Her eyes grow wide behind her magnifying glasses. 'Yes. I saw several people that day. Ian Christow, that doctor, he visited. So did the boy's babysitter, Sophie something-or-other. And there was another older woman there too. I'd never seen her before, but I heard later that she was a psychic, of all things.'

I haven't seen any of these people mentioned in the media articles I've found so far, though I think a psychic was mentioned somewhere. This investigation is going well. I already have three new suspects to look at!

'But Mark Reynolds was the main suspect. Wasn't he there that day?'

'No, I didn't see him that day.'

*Why was he the main suspect then?* 'Did you tell the police this?'

'Yes I did, but they wouldn't listen to an old lady. They decided he was guilty from the get-go.'

'Why were they so sure it was him?'

She shakes her head. 'I'm not sure, dear.'

'Is there anyone else in this street who might remember something?'

She stares into space, not answering, rigorously fiddling with her hair. It moves more than I expect and I realise that it's a wig.

I repeat the question.

'Sorry dear, I'm a bit vague today. No, Bill and I are the only ones still here. Everyone else has moved on I'm afraid.'

Shit. Still, I guess it's good that the local spy and gossip is still here.

'So, who do you think kidnapped Robin?'

She shakes her head. 'I *know* it was not Mark Reynolds, he was too nice. And he was at a public house all that afternoon, apparently, so there were many people able to vouch for him. I wouldn't be surprised if it was the doctor, especially since Jane broke it off with him. He might have been angry enough with her to do the worst thing you can do to a mother – take her child.'

'I haven't read anything about him in my research. Why did he and Jane break up?'

'The child mainly, from what I could tell. I think he wanted Jane all to himself and the boy was in the way, always drawing her attention away from him. That's probably why she ended it.'

'Is the doctor still in town?'

She shrugs. 'Perhaps. I don't go into town much these days, and I certainly wouldn't visit him.'

'All the reports only talk about Mark.'

'Mark wouldn't hurt a fly!' She sounds angry all of a sudden. 'Jane was an unfit mother. The house never looked clean. I cannot abide a dirty home, especially one with a young child living in it.'

I keep writing away in the notebook to distract me from the stabs of sadness I'm feeling. I take a deep breath. 'Do you know what happened to Jane? Did she stay in town?'

'I remember she moved out of the street after a year or so, and I never saw her again. But I don't get out much. Well, sometimes I . . .' she trails off mid-sentence. 'Sorry, what were you saying? I'm on strong medication. It sometimes makes me confused.'

'I'm sorry, do you want me to leave?'

'No, dear, I'm fine, really.'

'Okay. What about Mark?'

'Once he was named as a suspect, his reputation was shot. He lost his job. In the end, he packed up and moved, long before Jane did.'

I wonder where he went. I make a note to look him up on socials.

'So you think Dr Christow took Robin? What about the other visitors?'

She's getting flustered now. 'Maybe that babysitter? She was terribly fixated on Robin. Rumour has it that she was barren, but dearly wanted children.'

'You also mentioned an older woman, a psychic?'

'Yes. I don't know anything about her. I don't pay any mind to that mumbo jumbo.'

I sit back and look at my notes. One thing keeps nagging at me. 'So, what time did you last see Robin?'

She stares at me blankly. 'I don't remember now. He was there, and then he wasn't.'

I shift in the wicker chair awkwardly. 'Was he still there when Dr Christow visited? Or Sophie?'

She's zoning out again, hands fluttering. 'Of course, *they* weren't in the yard that day—'

'Esther, who's this?' A gruff voice suddenly interrupts her. I turn around to see an old man standing behind us with a hammer in his hand. He's bald, with a red-flushed face, wearing an old flannelette shirt and blue braces stretched over a big gut, holding up his pants.

Mrs Crale doesn't answer, so he points a thick finger at me. 'Who the hell are you?' he barks.

Shit, he's really annoyed. 'I'm doing a school assignment on the Robin Winter case. Mrs Crale agreed to answer a few questions.'

'Esther, go inside,' he says firmly. She stands up unsteadily.

He turns to me. 'My wife is ill. She doesn't need to be bothered, so rack off.'

I stand up too, pulling my shirt down where it has ridden up over my hips.

'I won't take up any more of your time, Mrs Crale. Thank you.'

Mr Crale steps onto the verandah, taking his wife by the elbow.

Just before I head back to the street, I stop and bring up a picture of Mum and Dad on my phone, turning the phone to Mrs Crale. 'Sorry, one last thing. Does this woman look familiar to you?'

Her eyes open wide, just for a moment, but she shakes her head.

I walk away, my heart beating fast in my chest. I'm almost out the gate when Mr Crale barks out to me.

'Do you go to Banville Street High School, boy?'

Shit, I never thought to look up the name of a local high school for my cover story.

'Yes,' I call back, hoping I sound confident.

As I cross the road, I hear the decisive bang of the front door.

\* \* \*

Kane and Shell are leaning on the car, eyes squinting in the sun, staring at their phones. At least they're not arguing.

Kane looks up. 'Get anything?'

'Maybe. She said Mark Reynolds couldn't have been the kidnapper because he was too nice and didn't visit the house that day. But she did offer some alternatives. There was some doctor that Jane dated, but he didn't like the attention she gave Robin. She mentioned a babysitter who she says became fixated on Robin, and she said the psychic that one of the news articles mentioned visited Jane that day too.'

Shell grins. 'That's good intel. We've gone from one suspect to four. Did she say anything else?'

'She said something like "they weren't there", but I don't know who she meant. It was like she was about to say something important but then her husband turned up and shut me down.'

Shell starts pacing around the car, hands clasped together behind her back, a parody of a TV detective.

'Okay, so if Mark didn't take Robin, that's one thing. But your Mum is claiming you were adopted, so why would someone take a kid and then put them up for adoption? If you took a kid you'd want to keep them, wouldn't you? Or ask for a ransom or something? It doesn't make any sense.'

'I'm not sure the adoption thing is even true.'

None of this makes much sense. It's like a black tunnel with no light at the end.

Shell rubs her closely cropped head.

'You should put sunscreen on that dome, it'll burn in this sun,' Kane snickers as he runs his hands through his own sweaty blond spikes, like he's in a shampoo ad.

'I'll get a hat,' she replies. There's something in Shell's face I can't read.

'You okay?' I ask, aware that we still haven't talked properly.

She glances at me, but deflects the question. 'Should we look at the creek back there? You said it was part of the investigation.'

'Sure,' I say.

The three of us walk up the street a bit to the next intersection and then turn left. The creek runs right along behind the houses for a few blocks before it curves away. There's only a footpath and a flimsy wooden guardrail separating it from the back fences. It's maybe ten or so metres across and quite full of water despite it being summer. It sure looks deep enough to drown in.

Kane eyes the creek apprehensively. It would be unsettling to someone who can't swim. 'You said they drained this or had divers or something?' he asks.

I nod. 'Yeah, police divers. I guess this is a logical kind of place to look for a missing kid.'

I can imagine a young Robin ending up here after wandering around on his own, curious and unsupervised. Or maybe he was trying to get away from someone? The creek is quite still today, but if it were on the move, it could be deadly if he fell in. There's something unsettling about the way it stretches out into the distance.

'Something we can ask the cop if we find him?' Kane says, tentatively. It's funny and kinda sad that he keeps adding in his thoughts here and there, trying to show that he can play detective too.

Shell sighs. 'This is morbid. We won't learn anything new here. Let's go to the *Courier* office, see what we can turn up on those other suspects.'

We climb back into the car and head back into town. I look back at the Winter house as it disappears behind us in the rear-view mirror. If the house didn't spark any memories, maybe nothing will?

Suddenly I remember Mr Crale's question, so I google the local schools. There's no Banville Street High School in Bellanta. Shit!

*Chapter 20*

# Headlines

The *Bellanta Courier* office is a bland old sandstone building just behind the main business strip in town. The tall exterior windows have blown-up front covers from past editions, proudly blaring headlines like 'War comes to Bellanta' and 'Local Mayor Honoured'.

We walk inside and up to the front counter where a girl wearing vivid eye makeup and a retro checked dress is typing away on an ancient computer.

'Hi, I called up here the other day and asked about looking at your archives.'

The girl nods and looks at something on her screen. 'Angus from Melbourne?'

'Yep.'

'You're lucky, we're only open today for a big meeting. You wanted files from 2010 onwards, right? I'll show you where the archives are. You need to be done by 3 pm sharp.'

I glance at my phone. It's 1.45 already.

'I've never been to Bellanta before, it's nice,' Kane says, flashing a smile at her. She doesn't respond and he looks a little disappointed. She indicates for us to follow her.

'Locals just call it Bell,' she replies in a bored monotone. Shell and I shoot a look at each other. *Bell?* That's what Dad said that last day.

She leads us into the public archive area, a room with lots of computers and a wall full of grey shelves she tells us are called compactuses. You have to crank these cool wheel handles like you're opening a bank safe to move them side to side. The compactuses house editions of the paper in special folders and boards that you can flick through.

'This section goes back to the start of 2010. Follow the instructions on how to search the records here,' she points to a laminated A4 sheet attached to the wall.

And with that she is gone.

I google Dr Ian Christow and find his general practice in Walker Street, not too far away. I wave my phone in the air. 'Hey, I've found the doctor. Let's go there next.'

Shell and Kane both give me a thumbs up.

We start flicking through the collection and soon we have a whole bunch of articles about the case.

Shell is a step ahead. 'Gus, let's take pics of these pages for now, then print them out later if we need to go over them properly.'

I nod. I'm trying to take in some of these headlines. 'Robin still missing', 'Police no closer to finding missing boy', 'Special squad from Sydney assist in missing boy case', and, worst of all: 'Police find no clues on missing Robin'.

Kane is just standing there, texting. I'm too focused to care.

Shell snaps a photo of each story as I find them. I keep wanting to stop and read them but she forces me to keep ploughing through ('We'll read them properly later'). After a while we form a rhythm. The same picture of Robin as a toddler that was used on the website is used in the articles, over and over. The photo starts out large in the earliest stories, but shrinks over time, just like the headlines. Same with the photos of Jane, both the happy 'before the kidnap' photo and the distressed 'after the kidnap' photo. Month by month the articles grow smaller and disappear from the front page to further back in the news section of the paper. I guess that's how it rolls. Big news becomes smaller news and then, after a while, it ceases to be news at all. Gone, like a dying star.

Annoyingly, there are no photos of Mark Reynolds or the other suspects. I guess if none of them were formally arrested, police wouldn't release their identities to the media. But they reported on Mark, so where did they get his name from?

At 3 pm on the dot, the girl from the front desk comes in. 'Time's up.'

Shell and I close the folder in front of us.

'We need an Officeworks to print out a bunch of articles and photos,' she says.

Kane gets googling. 'There's one a few blocks from here.'

We gather up our things and pile in to the car to head to Officeworks. We spend about fifteen minutes syncing Shell's phone with the machine. It costs like twenty bucks to print out all of the photos of the news clippings, but it's worth it. I also buy a fat bulldog clip so that I can keep them all in chronological order. Bundled together like this, it feels like I have a book in my hands that might be about me. We've found more than just stories about the crime itself. There's also interviews with neighbours, and appeals from the police asking for anyone who may have seen or heard anything in relation to the case to come forward. One article shows a missing poster on a telephone pole. It's like reading a crime novel, but there are no red herrings, no big reveal, just a string of facts and investigations – and then nothing. A story without an end.

I ignore a missed call from Mum and realise it's already after 3.30 pm.

'We should try and find the detective soon,' I say to Kane. He's on his phone again. 'Hello?'

'Gimme a minute,' he says gruffly.

'I need to try and find this guy today.'

Kane rubs his forehead and takes a long breath. He swipes away the text message he was reading and pulls up Google Maps.

'Google says the cop shop is on Tarcutta Street. Two minutes away.'

I turn to the back seat to ask Shell something, but she's staring out the window, into the distance. The sun is shining on her head and her eyes seem to be twinkling with purpose. Maybe it's just a trick of the light, but she seems different than she did even just a few days back.

The police station is a bland two-storey building with a pitched roof. It actually looks like a big house, except for the police sign and the three police cars and wagons outside in the carpark. I wonder how many cops work there and how many cells they have inside.

'How do you know he's even here at all?' asks Shell.

'I don't even know if he's still a cop. I just wanted to check here before trying to find his property.'

We pull up over the road and I walk into the station. At the desk I get complete déjà vu from when I went to the station in Hazleton. There's the same desk at the front, the same kind of posters on the wall. The officer at the desk is much older though, and he has the squarest chin in history.

I ask him about Firelli and get a disinterested answer. 'No mate, he retired coupla years back.'

I change tact. 'Does he still live out at Parkhurst?'

The officer peers at me suspiciously. 'Are you a relative?'

I shake my head and smile innocently.

'Privacy, mate. Can I help you with something? Do you want to report a crime?'

'No, thanks.'

I turn and leave before he can ask any more questions, feeling his eyes on my back as I go.

Back in the car, Kane finds Parkhurst on Google Maps. 'It's a bit out of town, so we better crack on.'

## Chapter 21

# Farmhouse

Fifteen minutes later we turn off the main road and onto a windy dirt road that's almost hidden in the trees. After five minutes of bouncing over potholes, we pull up outside an old farmhouse with 'Parkhurst' written on the letterbox in black Texta. It's a dishevelled building set back on a rough, overgrown piece of land. It looks like it's falling apart. The chimney might be the only thing holding the house up. The fence is rusty and the gate looks like it's hanging off its hinges in sheer exhaustion.

What a dump. Did Firelli buy this to do it up and just never get round to it?

I get out of the car, phone and notebook in hand.

'Want me to come with?' asks Shell, her eyes bright and eager.

I feel like I need to do this myself, so I tell her no, but thanks.

Kane smiles encouragingly and gives me the thumbs up.

I look over my list of questions to ask Detective Firelli. I've tried to group them into logical sections, themes of questioning. The list may be ordered but my head is all over the place. Between that and the file of printouts, I feel like I have a whole bunch of homework that someone needs to correct.

Will he have any answers? What if he won't tell me anything, and this is just another waste of time?

My phone buzzes with a text from Shell. It's a four-leaf clover emoji.

I walk up the rough dirt path to the scratched green front door. There's no doorbell so I knock tentatively. No answer. I knock more firmly. A chip of paint sticks to my knuckle.

'Hello? I'm looking for a Mr Frank Firelli.'

Nothing. I knock again. There's a sound of rustling and muttering from inside the house. Someone's in there. Probably loading a rifle to shoot me.

Suddenly the door swings open, revealing a strong but haggard-looking man standing in the doorway. No rifle at least. He's got a ratty grey beard and furious downward-sloped eyebrows, under a Holden baseball cap. He could be Firelli, but it's hard to tell behind the beard and cap.

'What do you want? You better not be selling Jesus, 'cos I'm not buying,' he grunts.

'I . . . I have some questions about an old case, and I wanted to speak to Detective Sergeant Frank Firelli—'

'Well, you've wasted your petrol. He doesn't live here.'

The door closes in my face. I stand there for a second, a bit thrown, then walk back to the car.

'No go, the bloke says Firelli doesn't live here.'

'Do you believe him?' Shell asks.

'I guess. Why would he lie?'

Shell frowns. 'Let's sit down with all these printouts. We need to plan our next move.'

I hop back in the front seat and Kane takes off down the road.

Was he there and just hiding out the back? Was that him at the door and he just didn't want to talk to anyone? If that was him, he sure looked different to the clean-shaved, slick detective that was the face of this case twelve years ago.

'Where to now?' Kane asks.

I shrug. 'I wanna go see that doctor, but his office won't be open this late.'

'We should find somewhere to stay, to get out of this heat. And we should get something to eat,' says Shell.

'I know just the place,' laughs Kane.

Shell shakes her head. 'Please don't suggest that shithole motor inn.'

# Chapter 22

# Karaoke

The Mountainside Inn is seventies brown brick, flat, squat, with a terracotta roof with strange curly trims. The sign boasts that it has eighteen rooms, a bottle shop and a restaurant called Foxy's Bar 'n' Grill. If this was a movie, this is where the serial killer would be hiding out, sharpening knives.

'Not a mountain in sight, so why the name?' Shell wonders out loud.

Kane shrugs. 'Who cares? It's the cheapest place in town.'

Yeah, it looks cheap all right.

We park to the side of reception and lumber inside. The woman behind the desk is like seventy, with this strange bunch of curly hair piled up vertically on her head, like a grey Marge Simpson.

'All I can give you is a double room for $70. It's another $25 for a roll-out bed,' she says. Her eyebrows are very high, too close to her hairline. Drawn on.

I really didn't think the money side through. I don't have much in the bank since Macca's payday isn't till next week. Hadn't really thought beyond visiting the house and finding Firelli. Too focused on me.

'We'll take it,' Shell hands over her credit card, which is very cool of her.

Kane had his hand on his wallet, about to pay before she chipped in. He's broke, I bet, after buying the Kingswood.

The room is tiny, with a double bed set against a vivid lavender wall. The roll-out bed is a tiny little stretcher that looks like it was meant for a child. Now I understand the descriptions of seedy motels I've read in books before.

'Me or Shell would break that, so I reckon the roll out is yours,' I say to Kane.

'Better than sleeping with either of you,' he says as he chucks his bag on the bed.

I pull out the big wad of printouts from my bag and start to work my way through them, sorting them into piles on the carpet, keeping an eye out for a clearer photo of Detective Firelli or even one of Mark Reynolds.

Shell is running her finger along the windowsill of the room, something I imagine Mum doing. No dust at least, judging by the look on her face.

'Stuff this,' says Kane, 'let's get something to eat. And drink.'

Shell nods. 'Yeah, this can wait a bit. And hey, that pub next door looks shit in either a retro way, or it's just straight-up shit. Let's check it out.'

The interior of Foxy's Bar 'n' Grill is stuck in time, like its name. There's red chequered curtains, dark wood and exposed brick everywhere. Long, worn-out bar. Only the fancy beer taps seem new. One good thing is that there is a cool old-fashioned jukebox in one corner, with actual records in it that flashes lights when someone chooses a song. Unfortunately, the jukebox is stuck in time too, judging by the ancient songs people are choosing.

There's about ten tables in front of the bar and a few poker machines against the back wall, making a ton of noise.

A sign at the bar says if you show your room key you can get five bucks off a main meal. This makes me feel slightly better. Kane grabs us a booth in the corner of the room and we all order a parma and chips. When the food comes out, mine just sits there. I eat a few of the chips, but I'm not hungry, which *never* happens. Shell and Kane eat mine for me.

Kane stands up. 'I'm going to get a few drinks for "me" and some soft drinks for you two. You guys can drink the extras when no one's looking, but don't get caught.'

Shell grins.

Despite the recent whiskey episode, drinking's never been my thing – but Kane and Shell seem to love it. Maybe it's because I've watched Mum drunk too many times? Right now though, I need something to turn off my head.

While Kane is at the bar, Shell and I study the customers closely. While the place is a motel, there's a sense that the bar is full of locals rather than out-of-towners. Shell turns back to me. 'One of these people could know something.'

Kane comes back from the bar, balancing two whiskey and cokes and a pint of beer. Shell grabs her glass from his hands. 'Or know someone who knows something. Whether it's Jane or Mark or that doctor or babysitter or even the psychic.'

Kane nods. 'Big crime in a small town.'

'Well, maybe, but it's not like I can just rock up over to the bar and ask if anyone knows anything, can I?' I say.

'Why not?' asks Shell. I can see she wants to stand up, but something is holding her back. She looks reluctant, which isn't like her. I'm just about to offer when Kane jumps up.

'Time for me to do some detective work. Plus, you underage kiddies need to lay low.' He laughs, but I feel like there's something deeper behind his joking.

'Good idea,' I say.

'I can talk sport with the guys and flash some muscle at the girls.' He grins.

Shell glares at him. 'Your gender roles are archaic, meathead.'

'Joking!' He winks at Shell and heads to the bar.

We watch him as he moves around, chatting to a couple of different people. The men eye him fairly suspiciously, but they seem to be talking to him, or at least not telling him to go away. He seems to win a few of the blokes over. Then he moves over to another part of the bar where several women are sitting together. He swaggers up to the table, looking at his watch. I swear he does that just so he can flex in front of them. He greets all of the women but soon it seems he's talking to one woman in particular.

'Is he picking up intel or just picking up?' Shell mutters. I can't tell either.

About ten minutes later, Kane comes back to the table, looking super smug.

'I have info.' Shell and I lean in close.

'That woman I was talking to, her sister is Sophie Baxter, Robin's old babysitter. She says Sophie still lives in town!'

Wow, that is big. 'Can we talk to Sophie?'

'Yep. She texted Sophie my number, so we might hear from her tomorrow.'

'Did she say anything else?'

'Just that Sophie knew Mark. She also knew that doctor and thought he was a dick.'

'Did she mention Robin at all?'

'Only when she mentioned that Sophie babysat him to help keep him away from Jane's customers.'

I guess that's something, right? I feel excited and sick at the same time.

We sit back and drink, watching the crowd, each of us in our heads a bit.

Shell is scratching at her black nail polish again.

'So, what's going on with you?' I ask.

She looks up at me, then knocks back her drink.

'Get me another one?' she says, waving her glass at Kane. After he ambles off, she turns back to me. 'It's weird. One day to the next, I don't know how I'm going to feel till I feel it.'

'I guess you can't talk to your parents until you figure this out for yourself first.'

Shell rubs the bridge of her nose with a shaky hand. She's taking in deep breaths, like I do when I get panicky. I think she's going to change the subject, but then she says, 'I actually did mention something about a made-up kid at school who was non-binary. Cheryl went on this super weird tangent and started to bang on about phases, experimenting, growing out of things.'

'Shit.'

'Yeah, not great. I'm sure she knew I was really talking about me.'

'Well, at the end of the day you're you and that's a pretty cool person to be.'

She smiles and gives me a quick kiss on the cheek, not something she's done before.

Kane returns with more drinks. He's been talking to the bartender, and it turns out that tonight is karaoke night. I can't think of anything worse than listening to other people butcher songs from the seventies and eighties, but an hour later we're all a bit tipsy and having a great time. Shell gets up and sings 'We Belong' by Pat Benatar at the top of her lungs. I think she's trying to channel Rebel Wilson from *Pitch Perfect*. And, in a strange kind of way, it works. The crowd is singing with her and not laughing at her. At the end of her song she calls me and Kane up to join her. Both of us shake our heads and try to look away. But she's persistent and soon she has the crowd chanting *Kane and Gus! Kane and Gus!*

Kane grabs my shoulder and pulls me out of my chair. 'Let's do it. You know you want to, deep down.'

He marches me to the stage to applause from the crowd.

Shell points to the screen. 'I chose this for us.'

Kane grins. I groan. Together we sing Queen's 'We Are The Champions'.

Later on we stumble back to the room and plonk ourselves on the bed, scattering all the printouts on the floor.

I sit there light-headed, looking at the missed calls and texts from Mum. I feel guilty, but I know that ringing her now, half drunk, would totally be a bad move.

Kane and Shell are arguing about *Doctor Who* being the best TV show in the history of creation. '*Doctor Who* broke new ground. There was nothing else like it back then, and there still isn't. All of time and space.'

Shell shakes her head. 'No way, it's so misogynistic. In some of the old episodes Gus has shown me, the Doctor's companion was like the only woman on the screen.'

'In new Who, the Doctor had a lesbian companion. And there was a woman married to a female Silurian, although not sure if it counts if she was a lizard . . .'

'I did like the female Doctor, especially her boots,' Shell admits.

I smile as they carry on, glad they're kind of getting on, then fall asleep.

# Chapter 23

# Doctor

I wake up late, my mouth drier than a desert. Shell and Kane are both snoring. He's on the roll-out, feet hanging off the edge. Shell's next to me on the main bed, hogging all the bedding.

I'm dying of thirst. I get out of bed slowly, accidentally stepping on the pile of *Courier* printouts we dropped everywhere last night. I start to sort them into piles, wondering if Sophie will have any answers.

Later that morning Kane drives us into the centre of town and we have a big breakfast at a local cafe. I have a huge pile of pancakes that makes me feel so full, but in a good way. Shell pays again, even though Kane and I try to. She's making good use of that new credit card.

'No text from Sophie yet?' I ask Kane.

He shakes his head. 'Let's go find this doctor.'

'We should have gone yesterday really. He's probably not open on a Sunday,' I say, wishing I'd thought of this earlier.

'Actually he is, I checked yesterday,' smirks Kane, 'but only till 12 so we better get going.'

Shell and I look at each other, impressed.

We climb into the Kingswood and Kane revs the engine like a hoon as we drive off.

Shell is hanging her head out the car window like a dog. 'So, this doctor isn't mentioned as a suspect in anything you've read so far, Gus?'

'He wasn't named, but that doesn't mean he wasn't in the frame at some point.'

'Ha, "the frame". Listen to you, just like a real cop,' snickers Kane. His voice gets a bit deeper suddenly, more serious. 'This isn't a game, y'know? It's not a movie like that stupid *Love, Simon* you watch all the time.'

'Yes, I know. But at the same time, it's like I'm being chased by a monster. I have to keep running or I'll be eaten.' It's half a lie. I'm too overwhelmed by the reality of what's happening. I have to keep it light and pretend this is a video game, that I have to keep moving up to the next level.

'Don't worry about monsters, mate. There's danger in the real world to look out for.'

'What do you mean?'

Shell gives Kane a death stare that shuts him up. Then she turns to me. 'We talked about this after you fell asleep last night. Someone took Robin and got away with it for years. They may still be in town for all we know. If they find out you're sniffing around the case, they won't be happy.'

'So you guys think I'm in danger?'

Kane opens his mouth, but Shell jumps in again. 'Solving this case will have consequences.'

They're right, of course. 'But what other option do I have? Forget I ever saw the website? Accept that I was adopted like Mum said and just pretend for the rest of my life?'

'You could let the police handle it,' Kane snaps. Why is he suddenly angry?

'I can't go backwards. I can't un-see that picture,' I say.

Shell sighs as Kane parks the car just outside the doctor's surgery.

I continue. 'And there's Robin. I've got to do this for him too.'

Kane turns to face me properly. 'But aren't you saying you *are* him?'

How do I answer this? 'Maybe I am. Maybe I'm not. I don't know anything anymore.' I really don't. I realise that I need to talk to Dr Yamada. Shit is getting weird.

Silence. I can't tell if he's still angry or if it's done now. He's a bit like that; he yells, then it's done and in the past.

'Maybe we should just go home?' Kane says.

Shell is rubbing the bridge of her nose again. I've seen her do this in tests, rubbing so hard I thought she'd give herself a nosebleed. 'I agree that Gus needs to be careful, but let's not give up yet. You've driven a long way to suddenly want to go home again, meathead,' Shell says.

'What did you call me, baldy?'

'You heard,' she replies.

Kane stretches out his arms, fingers entwined. He raises them above his head and flexes his biceps.

*Please don't say it.*

'Sun's out, guns out.'

Shell and I side-eye each other, groaning.

'Oh c'mon, I'm more than just muscles. I have a brain you know!'

'Sure you do. You just flexed your brain at us,' laughs Shell.

He laughs with her but it sounds forced. I suddenly realise that dropping out of school, working at Macca's and losing his footy status must really be bothering him. He's rubbing his knee again too.

'You better give that knee a stretch,' I say to him as I get out of the car. 'Is driving stuffing it up?' I don't want this trip to set back his physio progress.

'It's okay,' he says.

I keep thinking about what he said about danger. I guess I have been avoiding the idea that digging around this case could actually be dangerous. But I can't think about that right now. It's like for the first time ever I'm starting to see the whole storyline of my life, not just the chapters I was allowed to read. When I reach out my hand, I feel like I can touch the world in a way I couldn't before. I know it sounds wild, but I can almost feel changes permeating the air, like distant thunder on a white-hot summer day. I just need the courage to see this through.

Shell and Kane stay in the car while I walk into the doctor's surgery. It's not as sterile as others I've been to. There's a wall of posters and a heap of brochures on a table. Everything from nappy rash to constipation to mobility scooters. Life really, from beginning to end. There's only one person in the waiting room and she looks like she's at the death end of the spectrum. She's coughing like a barking dog.

The receptionist looks up with a friendly smile. She's maybe Mum's age, with blonde hair in a no-nonsense pony tail. 'Hello love. Can I help you?'

'Hi. I wanted to see if I could get an appointment with Dr Christow today please.'

'I'm sorry love, he's not in today. He only does every second Sunday. Dr Tundya has just had a cancellation at 11.30 though.'

Shit. 'No, it needs to be Dr Christow. When is he back in?'

'Tomorrow, but he's booked solid till Wednesday. Are you an existing patient?'

'Am I able to ring him? It's important.'

Her mouth flattens a little. 'Sorry love, I can't give out his number. Would you like to make an appointment for Wednesday or should I put you on his cancellation list?'

I am standing there silently, trying to figure out what to do next, when the old woman in the chair starts coughing again, even louder this time, like she's choking. The receptionist jumps up to help her. The woman is doubled over, wheezing as the receptionist tries to get her to sit up straight in the chair. Now's my chance, while she's distracted. I lean over her desk and look for something that might have Dr Christow's address or phone number on it. Luckily, a quick flick through the out tray reveals a letter to someone with his return address on the back: 94 Hastings Street, Bellanta.

I memorise the address and turn back to the receptionist, who is helping the old lady. 'Can I help?'

'Grab her some water will you?' She points to a water cooler. I fill a cup and hand it to the old woman.

'Just a sip love,' says the receptionist encouragingly.

Not sure what else to do, I leave, repeating the address over and over in my head.

When I tell Shell and Kane, they're not impressed.

Shell's shaking her head. 'What use is his address if we don't know where he is?'

'His receptionist said he's not working today, so he might be at home. I feel like we're running out of time. Mum's rung again. I'm afraid she'll call the police and they'll make us go home, and then it's all over. I feel like this is my only chance to get answers. Like, right now, literally this weekend.'

Shell sighs. Kane shrugs and googles directions to Hastings Street.

The doctor's house is on the outskirts of town, on a very quiet street, surrounded by bushland at the back and with a thick hedge fencing all four sides of the property. There's a small gate in the middle at the front. I figured a doctor would have a fancy house, especially in the country. It's modern and sleek, like it's been pulled out of a brochure.

Kane turns off the engine. 'I'll wait here. I can't see a car anywhere but you should still knock on the door and see if someone's home first.'

Shell and I walk up to the front door and ring the bell. 'If someone answers I'll ask for directions or something,' I whisper.

'Who needs directions when you have Google Maps?'

'I'll say my phone is dead.'

Nobody comes to the door.

'You stay here in case someone comes. I'll have a snoop round the back,' I say to Shell.

'Huh? What are you looking for?'

'Dunno. Mrs Crale seemed quite sure he was a strong suspect.'

I walk around the side of the house to a pretty empty backyard. There's a large pile of firewood sitting next to a set of cellar doors that seem to lead directly underneath the house. They have menacing padlocks on them. Creepy.

Suddenly a car horn blares. Kane?

Then I hear someone behind me. I freeze.

'Gus, it's time to go.' It's Shell, looking worried. She scared the shit out of me. 'A Lexus just pulled up out front. We have to leave, *now*!'

We start making our way back to the front yard. There's a tall, clean-shaven man in his early forties in a tailored blazer and expensive-looking jeans standing on the path to the front door. He has shiny black hair, stylishly slicked back, and dark sunglasses. He's jiggling a set of keys in his hand.

His head jerks up in surprise. 'Who the hell are you?' he says in a cold voice.

I gasp, dropping my notebook and stumbling to pick it up. Shell strides up to him and holds out her hand. 'Dr Christow? I'm Michelle Oliver and this is Angus Green. We're doing an assignment for school and someone said you would be a good person to talk to.'

He looks us up and down suspiciously. 'What were you doing in my yard?'

Shell doesn't flinch. 'We tried the front but there was no answer, so thought we'd try the back door before we left.'

She is amazing. I would have just stood here panicking.

He frowns at her. 'I don't have time to talk to you. I'm busy.'

'We only have a couple of quick questions.'

I finally find my voice. 'It's about the kidnapping of Robin Winter. Back in 2010.'

Dr Christow stops jiggling his keys and stands very still. He takes his sunglasses off, revealing deep brown, kinda dead eyes. 'I don't have time to talk to you. Leave.'

Somehow, I find the courage to stand my ground. My mouth is dry.

'You dated Jane Winter?'

'So?' His nostrils flare a little.

Shell takes over. 'We're interested to find out what she was like, get the human side of the story. All the coverage focused on the crime, but there was very little about Jane and what she was like. For example, was she a nice person?' .

His face softens slightly. 'Yes.' He reaches into his pocket, taking out a pack of cigarettes. 'You have three minutes,' he says, lighting one with a practiced flick. Weird to see a doctor smoke.

I open my notebook and start to scribble some notes, as much to avoid his intimidating stare as anything.

'Was she a good mother?' Shell asks.

He nods. 'She was okay. The papers were happy to paint her as a bad mother because it suited their agenda. She used to get a bit overwhelmed – she was trying to run a business *and* look after a sooky kid.'

I wipe my brow. 'Did you get on well with Robin?'

Christow grimaces. 'He was a little shit. He cried all the time, sucking up all her attention.'

I catch my breath. This is hard to hear. Shell gives me a reassuring smile.

'Sounds like things were easier when Robin wasn't around.' she says.

He eyes her suspiciously. 'In some ways yes. But losing him broke her into pieces.'

Poor Jane.

'Where were you the day Robin was taken?' I ask.

'I was at work, all day. It was only that night that I found out what had happened.'

*That's not what Mrs Crale said.* Shell pushes him a little. 'I read an article that you were at the house that day.'

He sneers, his mouth forming a mean slit. He answers carefully. 'Yes, it's true that I was there that day, *briefly*. My receptionist received a call from Jane saying she needed to see me urgently. I thought it was odd that she didn't call my mobile, but I went over anyway. There was no answer when I arrived, and she didn't pick up when I rang, so I went back to work.'

'If Jane didn't call you, then who did?' asks Shell.

'It turned out she hadn't called me. She had been taking her afternoon nap. Like I told the police back then, clearly someone was trying to implicate me in this crime.'

'So what time were you at the house?'

'Around 4 pm.'

'And Robin wasn't in the yard then?'

'No.'

'Who do you think took Robin?' I ask.

His face goes red and his fingers grip tighter on his keys. 'That Reynolds freak.'

'But he had a strong alibi, so it couldn't have been him, could it?' I say.

Christow glares at us. 'I don't know. Probably that clingy, intense babysitter. She was always trying to find excuses to look after Robin, just so she could have the kid to herself. Word is that she couldn't have kids of her own. Not being able to have kids *does not* make you a kidnapper, but she sure behaved like she was obsessed with that kid.'

'Anyone else you can think of?'

'Not really. Unless maybe that Lemarchant woman, the psychic. I believe she was a customer of Jane's.' He uses air quotes for 'psychic'.

Shell clears her throat. 'Sounds like you didn't like any of them very much.'

Christow frowns, but he looks sad, somehow. 'I couldn't stand them. If Mark had left her alone, I could have helped her turn her life around, but he kept hanging around. He said it was just about looking after the kid, but he just didn't want anyone else dating her. Same with Sophie. At least she had a function, gave us some space. And as for the psychic, well . . . the point is, if they had all kept their noses out of it, I never would have ended it with Jane.'

He stubs out his smoke on the ground.

'I thought Jane ended the relationship?' says Shell.

He raises his hand in a 'stop' gesture. 'That's more than enough for your assignment.'

'Were you questioned by police, back then?' I ask.

'Yes. Now, get out before *I* call the police.'

I look at Shell. Neither of us move.

'*GO!*' he yells.

We rush to the gate and onto the road where Kane is parked,

engine running. We jump into the back seat, adrenalin overflowing.

Kane stares at us. 'What happened? What did he say?'

Christow has followed us out and is standing by his jet-black Lexus, watching us closely. He's clearly not moving till we're gone.

'Let's go back to the motel first, so he can see we've gone.' Kane takes off. In the rear-vision mirror I can see Christow staring at us, arms crossed and scowling, until we turn the corner.

* * *

Back at the motel, we explain what happened to Kane.

'Basically, he was very suspicious of us and threatened to call the cops if we didn't leave.'

Kane shrugs. 'Well, to be fair, you were creeping around his house.'

'That's true. But it does feel we rattled him a bit,' says Shell.

'He's definitely a key suspect,' I say.

Shell lays back on the bed. 'If Reynolds didn't do it, then this guy is a strong possibility. He seems dangerous. Bad-tempered. He might have been shitty with Jane for ending their relationship. He may have wanted to punish her.'

'I wonder if he's mentioned in any of this lot?' I start thumbing through the articles again. I notice that Kane is busy texting, not really listening. I realise that Mum hasn't called or texted today.

'Who have you been texting all this time?'

'No one,' he says, red-faced.

'What do you think about Christow?'

He scratches his head. 'If this Christow bloke did it for whatever reason, then what did he do with Robin? Why take him yet stay in town?'

*Maybe he killed Robin.* I sure don't want to say that out loud. I shake my head. 'I don't know. But if he's telling the truth, then who asked him to the house?'

Kane shrugs. 'But if he did do it, you've just shown your hand, Goose.'

Shell and I look at one another. He's right.

'We should have said we were collecting for charity or something.'

'Maybe, but that would have just got a door shut in our faces,' says Shell. 'Anyway, it's done now, so let's see what we can find in all these papers.'

She smiles at me, a weak 'it'll be okay' smile.

We all sit on the bed and try to set out what we have into piles again. It takes ages. Every now and then we put one aside for later reference, but mainly we just have lots of articles with the same information. As we go, we cross reference the reports against the stuff I've written in my notebook so far, to see if they line up.

Kane holds up a page. 'Here's a better pic of Firelli.' He hands the printout over to me and I study it closely. There's something about the eyes and the shape of his eyebrows . . .

'I reckon that guy at the house *was* him, just older and with a beard. We should go back.'

'Why would he lie? Why not just tell you to piss off?' Shell asks.

'Meth lab?' jokes Kane as he rearranges some of the pages.

Shell pulls out another printout. 'Hey, that psychic, Anna Lemarchant, is mentioned here. The journalist claimed she was trying to drum up business by inserting herself into the case.'

'Mrs Crale and Christow both mentioned her. I think he suggested that maybe she took Robin so she could then offer to "find" him using her "powers", to prove to the town that she wasn't nuts.'

'That's a batshit thing to do,' Kane says.

'Yeah, but you never know. Maybe she was just wacky?'

'Or maybe she's the real deal and her spirits told her something? She could be worth following up,' says Shell, googling Anna.

I turn to ask Kane if we can go back there but he's mysteriously disappeared. I don't know what he's up to. Or who he's up to it with.

Suddenly he reappears, holding up his phone. 'That text from Sophie just turned up.'

## Chapter 24

# Babysitter

Kane calls Sophie right away, a serious look on his face. 'Yes, that's right, the guy who spoke to your sister. My friend Gus and I are doing a school assignment and we'd love to talk to you, seeing you knew Jane and Robin.'

Sophie invites us to come over in an hour. I re-read my notes as we get ready. I hope this goes better than our talk with Christow.

She lives on the rougher side of town by the look of the houses. They remind me of home. Is it still home? My life back in Hazleton seems a million miles away and it's only been two days. I check my phone. Mum hasn't called today. I'm relieved, but feel guilty at the same time. I just can't deal with her right now.

'Kane, I think Gus and I should go in, not you. Two blokes turning up might spook her a bit,' Shell says from the back seat.

'Nah, no way.' He shakes his head. 'I got this lead.'

Shell wisely plays up to his ego. 'I know you did, but I think if you're there, she'll just stare at you.' I'm sure he sees through it, but he agrees anyway.

Sophie's yard is full of neglected grass, with big cracks in the footpath and heaps of weeds. It's so different to Mrs Crale's garden full of roses, or Dr Christow's neat yard. The entire house is painted an odd blue – even the window frames. It was like blue paint was going cheap so they did the whole house with it.

I knock on the door and a woman in her thirties answers. She's wearing a long black cardigan that hangs almost to her ankles over a plain T-shirt and cut-off shorts. Her red hair is tied up on top of her head in a loose bun and she has glasses on. She is pretty but she looks sleepy. 'Are you Kane?'

'Gus and Shell actually, Kane is, um, busy. Hi Sophie.'

She nods and opens the old flyscreen door. It has a nasty hole in it. She must see me looking, because she mutters something about fixing it as she leads us into the lounge room. All her furniture looks like it came from an op-shop, but the room is clean. I'm surprised. I thought it would be a dump, judging from outside.

She makes us a cup of instant coffee, and then sits in the chair opposite us, her legs tucked under her and her big cardigan wrapped around her like a cocoon.

'Alright then. You wanted to know about Jane and Robin Winter?'

'Yes.' I was going to roll out the lie Kane told her about a school assignment, but I guess I don't need to.

'Right. My sister says there might be a reward for information on Jane? I could do with the cash right now.'

Shell is squirming in her seat. 'Kane might have *implied* there was a reward, but there isn't,' she mutters. He could have mentioned this earlier!

'That's a shame.' Sophie goes to stand up.

*Shit.* 'This is a school assignment, but we're really keen to find out more about the case, to see if we can find out the truth for Robin. You used to babysit him, didn't you?'

Cautiously Sophie sits back down. She wraps her arms around her knees. 'Robin was a gorgeous baby, utterly precious. But Jane struggled to look after him sometimes.'

'Why did she struggle?' I ask, flicking to a new page in my notebook.

'Robin cried a lot, more than other kids, and she couldn't cope with him on her own. Plus, as you no doubt know, she was selling weed, and she was worried that she'd be arrested. Honestly, I was a lot better at caring for him than she was.'

Creepy thing to say.

'What about Mark Reynolds?' asks Shell.

Sophie's face clouds over. 'They dated for ages. He helped her when she gave birth.' Sophie sighs. 'Look, Mark started out nice enough, but once Robin was born, he got controlling. He wanted her to move in with him, be a proper little family. He was a bit obsessed with this idea of a family. Turns out he'd grown up in and out of foster homes. He was worried that she'd be caught and Robin would be taken away by social services. So was I, if I'm honest.'

She pulls her cardigan tighter around herself. 'I looked after Robin at lot and he *loved* me. We had such fun. I treated him like he was my own.'

Shell and I exchange a quick look. 'Was Mark worried enough about Robin being taken off Jane to kidnap him?' I ask.

Sophie fiddles with her bun. 'No, he loved Robin. Mark taking him never made sense to me.'

'Do you know what happened to Mark?' I ask.

'No idea. Being a suspect ruined his reputation, so he just had to leave and start again somewhere else. Jane left town too, maybe a year later.'

Wow. Jane just left?

'Do you know where she went? Do you still have a number for her, or an address?' I sound desperate.

'I don't know. I probably have an older number in my phone. No idea if it still works.'

I catch my breath as she scrolls through her contacts. 'Yep, here we go.'

I'm shaking as she takes a post-it and a pen from the coffee table and scribbles the number on it for me. I want to call right now, but I have to stay calm and keep going.

'So you really liked babysitting Robin?'

She takes off her glasses, her eyes a little misty. 'Yes. He was such a sweetie. That little boy being taken from her, from all of us, is just horrific.' She goes quiet for a moment.

Shell nudges me. 'Do you have kids?' she asks in a gentle voice.

'No,' says Sophie, quite loudly. 'But I could if I wanted to. There was a rumour . . . I don't know who started it, but it was cruel. And implying I may have taken him . . . Jesus!'

She takes a sip of her coffee before continuing in a slightly calmer voice. 'I remember I went to see Jane a week after it happened. She was a wreck. She kept asking me who would take him. She couldn't believe no one saw anything.'

I take a breath, remembering Christow's response to this question. 'And you were there on the actual day he was taken, weren't you?'

She stares at me like I've just farted on her couch.

'Who told you that?' She's almost yelling. I can see why Christow called her intense.

I try to look innocent. 'I think I read it somewhere.'

She shakes her head. 'Well, I was sort of there. I got a text asking me to come and look after Robin for an hour or so. But when I arrived, Jane didn't answer the door. I banged on the door again, rang her, called out – but no joy. So I left.'

Sounds like the same thing that Christow claimed happened to him. Was she being set up too? Or was she lying?

'Did the text come from Jane's phone number?'

'Not her usual one, but she had a couple of different phones, for "business" reasons, y'know, so I never questioned it at the time.'

Makes sense I guess. 'What time was this?'

'Around 4.30-ish?' Sophie sighs. 'Anyway, it turned out that Jane never sent that text.'

There's a pattern emerging here.

She shakes her head. 'Poor Jane. She was a broken woman after he was taken. The police even accused her of killing him at one stage. Just to test the waters, I think. But it shattered her to think someone might think she could do that to her own beautiful baby.'

Shell leans forward. 'Sophie, who do you think took Robin?'

'I've wondered that so many times over the years. Like I said, I don't think it was Mark.'

'Someone mentioned that Jane was dating a doctor?' Shell's guiding her now.

'Oh yes, Christow. He was a smarmy prick. Still is.'

'Is he a likely suspect?' Shell continues.

'Absolutely. Jane used to have a nap every afternoon at 3 pm, so I felt it had to be someone who knew that Robin would be on his own at that time of day. Christow would know that.'

'Insider knowledge,' I say. I had never thought of this before.

'Yes. Plus, Jane broke it off with him because she was scared of him.'

'She did? What was she scared of?'

'She said that he'd wanted Robin out of the way so he and Jane could spend more time alone. I ended up doing a lot more babysitting once he was on the scene. I was happy to, not just for the money, but to keep Robin safe.'

'Safe? Was he in actual danger from him?' Shell asks.

Sophie sounds angry, eyes ablaze. 'Yes. He hurt Robin once. When Jane and I saw what he'd done, she ended it.'

I feel sick.

'Anyone else you can think of?' Shell asks, one eye on me.

'Maybe that loopy Anna had something to do with it? She was

a good customer of Jane's, if you know what I mean, but not her friend. After Robin disappeared she was all over Jane, trying to get her time in the spotlight, making out she was her best friend, and that they were both "spiritual". Sophie looks up, frowning. 'Anna was just nuts enough to do it.'

'Pity she couldn't help find him with her powers,' I say softly, to see what reaction I get.

Sophie laughs, too loud. 'The only power she has is the power to be the centre of attention. Bloody show pony.'

Does Anna taking him make sense?

Sophie flicks her eyes to a clock on the wall. 'Is that it? I need to get back to the books.'

'Books?'

'I'm studying to be a social worker. Big assignment due next week, so I have to pull my finger out.'

I'm desperate to get out of there and ring Jane's number.

'If I help you solve this, I want some of the reward,' she calls out in a I'm-joking-but-I'm-not-joking voice as we leave.

Kane's busy texting again when we climb back into the car. He looks up, almost guilty. What's up with him?

'Thanks for telling her sister about some non-existent reward, you fraud,' Shell pokes Kane in the bicep.

He looks away from her guiltily. 'I thought it might help her talk?'

Only half listening to them, I twist the phone number round and round between my fingers. It might be the missing piece or a dead end.

Shell grabs my hand and stops my nervous twisting. She takes the post-it from me and slaps it on her forehead, like when we play Celebrity Heads.

'Ring the number. Tell whoever answers about our "school assignment" and that you're trying to track down Jane Winter.'

She gives me an encouraging smile. Kane hands me my phone. I carefully type in the number and hit the call button before I can overthink myself into a coma.

All the breath goes out of the car, like in an airlock. Time stops and reality caves in on itself. I can feel myself about to have a panic attack.

What if Jane actually answers? What will I say?

*The number you have called has been disconnected. Please check the number and try again.*

# Chapter 25

# Psychic

I don't even know that I expected the number for Jane to work, if I'm honest, but it's still a real let-down.

I'm feeling exhausted, worn-out emotionally. I'm not sure how many more times I can listen to stories of Jane's struggles and Robin's neglect without losing my shit altogether.

'Okay, what now? Go back out to the cop's property?' Kane asks, tapping his fingers on the steering wheel.

Shell hushes him. 'I've found the psychic's website.' She passes me her phone. Anna's number is listed under an ad for crystal healing. I ring her up. A gentle, soothing voice answers. '*Hello.*'

'Hi. Um is this Anna Lemarchant, the psychic?'

'*Yes, I help people connect with the spirit world.*'

'My name is Angus and I'm interested in a thingy, a reading?'

'*I read palms, tarot and auras, and conduct crystal therapy. Which would you like?*'

'Which one is cheapest?'

'*A palm reading is $40, and a full psychic reading is $150,*' her voice is less soothing now, a little impatient.

'I'll take a palm reading then. Are you free today?'

'*Well, I usually only do readings on—*'

I can tell she's going to say no, so I cut her off. 'Please, I really need some guidance today.'

I hope a bit of emotional blackmail works for her. Mum uses it on me every day. Well, until recently.

Anna gives in and tells me to come over at 3.30 pm. She gives me the address.

'Do I make out I'm some random customer? Or give her the school assignment story? Or do I tell her the truth?' I ask.

Shell is fanning herself with a flattened-out chip packet. 'I think you should just go to her and say nothing. Let her do her thing. Don't tell her anything is right, even if she gets something right. In fact, tell her it's all wrong. Then, while she's a bit thrown by this, ask her about her work with the police.'

Kane nods in agreement. 'Shell's right, make her work first. Then hit her with questions.'

It sounds like a plan.

So at 3.30 pm I'm walking up the path to her door. Her house is a simple weatherboard place, quite close to the main street. Very ordinary, not covered in dream weavers and all the things I associate with psychics or fortune tellers on TV. The doorbell is an actual bell on a chain, with two crystals hanging above it. It gives out this warm, oddly comforting kind of chime when I ring it. A minute later Anna appears. She is surprisingly short, but with a commanding presence. She's about sixty, and has this incredible face, with dark, dynamic eyes, and short, wavy grey hair. She's wearing a plain green shirt and jeans. I don't know what I expected exactly, but she is not it. She totally looks normal.

'Come in Angus,' she says in that soothing voice. She opens the door and gestures inside. I step into the light hallway and she points me through a door to a room with a round table topped with a purple and gold cloth, a huge mug and a pack of tarot cards. 'Did you want some ginger tea?'

I say no and sit in the chair that she pulls out for me before sitting down herself.

The room is airy and nice, with feathers of different sizes all arranged on one wall. It smells of patchouli oil. Given Sophie said Anna was a good customer of Jane's, maybe it's to cover up the smell of weed.

'I've never done anything like this before,' I say.

She smiles. 'I thought so.'

Well, she would say that, wouldn't she.

'Using palmistry to predict the future has been around for centuries. The physical features of our hands are like a blueprint. We just need to know how to read it. It's nothing to be scared of.'

She takes my right hand and examines it. Her hands are soft and delicate.

'There are different hand shapes. Yours is a water shape, because of your long fingers. This means that you are a compassionate person.'

I take it all in silently, trying to keep my face neutral.

She runs her finger across my palm, pointing areas out. 'Here is your mount of Saturn. Yours is quite large, which shows that you have wisdom but also fortitude, that you've been through some ups and downs.'

I want to roll my eyes, but I have to admit she's starting to intrigue me.

'You said you needed guidance . . . is there something in particular I can help with?'

I shake my head. 'No. I'm happy for you to just tell me what you see.'

She nods. 'Your headline is quite deep, which means that you are a complex person, but it is broken in places,' she points out two places on my hand that I've never noticed before. 'This shows that you're experiencing mental strife. I imagine that's what brought you here today.'

I say nothing.

'Now, your heartline is this one here. It's quite faint, so it looks like you aren't in love right now, but you can see that it gets deeper later on, so there is love coming for you one day.'

'When?' I ask. I can't help myself.

She frowns, holding my hand closer to her face. 'Next Monday.'

I look at her in surprise and she laughs. 'I'm joking, it seems to be a while away yet.'

'Now let's have a look at your lifeline . . .' she trails off. 'How interesting.'

'What?'

'You seem to have two lines. See here. Two shallow lifelines running parallel before they merge and become one much deeper line.'

I snatch my hand away. Can she really see all this?

She clasps her hands together in her lap, unperturbed. 'You seem to be experiencing life on two levels. Whatever you are searching for, you will find it when these two lines converge. Once that happens, you will have a great path in life.'

It sounds like she might know what she's talking about, but it has to be a scam, doesn't it? It's time to get onto what I really came her for.

'Can I ask you something unrelated, please?'

She looks puzzled. 'Go ahead.'

I take out my notebook and pen. 'You offered to help the police during the Robin Winter case in 2010, didn't you?'

She leans back in her chair, the softness in her face falling away like mud thrown at a wall. 'Why are you asking about that?'

I roll out the lie about the school assignment. 'I read an article that said you told the police that you had a sense of what had happened. Is that true?'

She stares at me with those curious dark eyes. 'Why should I tell you?'

'I'm genuinely interested in what happened to Robin.' *You don't know just how interested I am.*

She studies my face for a minute. 'If you pay me for a full reading, I'll answer your questions. A gal's gotta earn a living.' She grins, but there's something creepy behind her smile.

I nod, hoping I have that much left in my wallet. 'I have about $90 in cash.' Only because Shell keeps paying for everything.

'That will do then,' she says, settling back into her chair. 'I still remember it quite vividly. I knew Jane a little. We did some business together. She was a good person but she had bad energy around her. People trying to control her, to change her ...' she lowers her voice. 'Anyway, I dreamed one night of a lost child, underground, crying out for his mother. It was such a powerful dream that I woke up convinced it was corporeal. That morning I heard the news about Robin being taken and I felt like my dream was actually a vision. After I had the same dream the next night, and the night after, I went to the police and offered my help.'

'What did they say?'

Her nostrils flare. 'They laughed at me and told me to leave.' There's a vein pulsating above her right eye. This clearly still bothers her, even after all this time.

'So what did you do next?'

'I went to the *Courier* and offered my help to the journalist there who covered crime and court cases. He was no better than the police. Worse, in fact, because he wrote about my offer and made me look like a crank.'

I feel a bit sorry for her. 'That was shitty. Did you keep having the dream?'

She nods. 'Every night for weeks. I started to dread going to bed knowing that it would come.'

'And always the same dream?'

'Yes, always.'

I shudder, remembering the cellar doors I saw at Dr Christow's house.

'Did you ever have any idea where *exactly* Robin was?'

'Once or twice, I was sure I heard the town hall clock in the distance. It has a very distinctive sound. I felt he was still alive, and still in town.'

I remember hearing that unusual chime the day we arrived.

'So the police and the newspaper didn't believe you. What did you do next?'

She starts fiddling with her hair.

'I went to his mother, Jane. She was all over the place, poor thing. I wanted to comfort her with the knowledge that I thought Robin was still alive. I think it helped. I gave her a tarot reading. We lit candles and sought guidance from the spirits. We did everything to try to find out more, but nothing came. I badly wanted to help her.'

Jane must have been desperate to believe in this shit. But I guess if your kid is taken, you would try anything to get them back.

'Did the police know you were talking to her?'

'Yes. The main detective running the show, Firelli, was a pig. He told me to leave Jane alone. And Jane's ex was furious. They had a big fight over it.'

'You mean Mark Reynolds? Why did he get angry?'

She stares directly into my eyes. It's unsettling. 'He knew something, I know he did. He wasn't who he seemed to be. I could see through his veil, and he knew it.'

'What do you mean?'

'Just that. He tried to seem like one person but he was actually another. His whole persona seemed like a costume. Underneath I saw a man who could be ruthless and cunning.'

I keep getting different views of Mark from different people. Mrs Crale said he was nice, Christow said he was weird, Sophie said he was decent. Now this . . .

'Do you think he took Robin?'

She pauses for what seems like a solid minute. We sit there, staring at one another.

'Yes. I'm sure of it.'

'Did you tell Jane that?'

'I tried to, in a roundabout way, but she didn't believe me. She got upset with me, and stopped talking to me for a while.' She pauses, eyes narrowed. 'You never wanted a reading at all, did you?'

Caught. I figure I have nothing to lose by being a bit more honest with her.

'No, I didn't. I just had this idea that I could solve this by talking to people who were there at the time.'

She looks angry.

'I'm sorry, I didn't think you'd talk to me if I told the truth,' I stammer.

She holds out her hand. 'I'd like that payment now, before you ask any more questions.'

I take the cash out of my wallet and hand it over. Anna counts the notes quickly before looking up at me again and nodding.

'So, when did the dreams stop?'

'About two months after he was taken. At first I worried that it meant Robin was dead, but I never got that sense at all.'

'What do you think happened to him?'

'I wondered if his captor had taken him out of town perhaps. I had the feeling that his energy was far away, but not gone, not dead,' she sighs, holding out her hands in a gesture of resignation. 'I don't know. It was a long time ago now.'

She seems to snap back into the present, running her fingers through her hair dramatically. 'Why did you choose this case in particular for your assignment?'

'No reason. Do you know Dr Christow?'

Her head moves to the side a little, like a curious bird.

'Why are you asking about him?'

'Could he have taken Robin to punish Jane?'

She laughs at this, but it's an empty kind of laugh. 'His arrogance was off the charts, so maybe, but it's such an extreme act.'

'Can you think of anyone else with a motive?'

She pauses, considering her answer. 'Jane's babysitter Sophie was head over heels for Robin. She was far too attached. I suppose it's possible that Sophie took him. She had a *very* intense energy.'

'Was there ever a sense of who was with Robin in your dreams, of who took him?'

'I could feel a presence around him, but I never saw anyone else in my dreams. If only—'

I'm not sure if I should say it or not, but I do anyway.

'Weren't you at the house that day?'

I brace feet my on the floor, as if I'm about to be hit by a wave of psychic fury that might knock me off my chair. She stares at me, head on an angle again. Is it surprise? Fury? Disbelief? I genuinely can't tell. Her face wears all of those expressions, yet none at the same time.

'Who told you that?'

'I read somewhere that you took him so that you could use your powers to rescue him.'

She starts laughing. A snigger at first. Then deeper, before she breaks into full-on mad laughter.

'Well, if that's true, my plan backfired!'

She stops laughing suddenly. Creepy. 'I went over that day, to pick up something from Jane, but she wasn't answering the door, so I left. I was there for maybe two minutes, and that cost me dearly. I was interviewed by the police. Once I had been labelled a suspect, my offer to help looked ludicrous. It was an awful time.'

She stares right into my eyes. I'm spooked by her intensity. 'Do *you* think I took him? Is that why you're—' she grabs both my hands, gasping, and stands up suddenly. 'Are you Robin?'

I feel a wave of panic hitting me. She isn't the right person to tell, not yet.

'No! You've got your wires crossed there.' I pull my hands from hers.

It feels like she's staring into my heart or my soul or something, I dunno. She seems to settle again. 'Sorry, I don't know what came over me. But just for a moment . . .'

This is way too weird.

'I have to go. Thanks for the chat and the reading.'

'Make sure you mention that I'm not a fake in your assignment. I could have helped back then if people had let me.'

I nod and head for the door. As I walk down the path, I feel her eyes on me.

'My dreams mean something, remember that,' she calls. I turn back, but she's gone.

# Chapter 26

# Detective

Back in the car, I tell Shell and Kane what happened, shuddering when I tell them about the moment where she thought I was Robin.

'Spooky,' Kane says. 'Wonder where that came from?'

'Maybe her powers are real after all?'

Shell's shaking her head. 'She's fishing, that's all, looking for a reaction.'

'Well, it worked!' I say. 'But she agrees that Sophie was obsessed with Robin and that Christow is up himself. And she said Mark was pretending to be someone else, if only we knew what that even meant.'

Kane is busy texting someone *again*. I'm super curious now. I point at the top corner of his windscreen. 'Is that a crack up there?' While Kane is distracted, I snatch his phone out of his hand.

'Give that back!' he barks.

'Who you been texting all day? Is she from school or Macca's?' When I look at the screen my jaw drops.

'Kane, what the hell? You've been texting my mum!'

He grabs the phone back, red-faced. 'She's worried about you,' he says sheepishly.

I trust him with so much. I never expected this. How could he? 'Traitor!'

'We're both worried. You're playing with fire, Goose.'

I'm so angry I can almost feel my blood boiling. 'How could you do this behind my back?'

Kane's cocky demeanour has slipped to the floor next to his expensive runners. 'I'm sorry, but I'm just looking out for you. I'm not telling her anything about the case, just that you're okay.'

I shake my head in disbelief. 'Did she force you to do this?'

'No! She's been helping me with something and I owed her.'

'What has she been doing for you?' My mind is going *way* too many places with this.

'Nothing, it's no big deal. I just owe her, that's all.'

I can't process this right now. It's too much to take in. It does explain why Mum hasn't been calling or texting as much today. Clearly she's had a direct line to what's been going on.

'Let's just go,' I say.

'Right.' He starts the car, revving it a bit too hard.

In the rear-vision mirror, Shell is watching us with a curious look on her face. I turn to her as we drive off. 'Did you know he was doing this?'

She shakes her head. 'No. But you really could be in danger. We *all* could be.'

She does look concerned, in a way I haven't seen before. I barely thought about myself being in danger, let alone the two of them. I've dragged them into this without stopping to consider the consequences, just like Dad. The thought that they could get into trouble or be hurt by this is overwhelming.

We sit in silence the whole drive to Parkhurst.

'It's funny that there were these ready-made suspects. But if this was a movie, the twist would be that the kidnapper is someone else entirely, someone we haven't considered,' Shell says as we pull up.

'Like who?' I ask, getting out of the car.

'Dunno,' she shrugs. 'Want us to come with this time?'

I shake my head and walk to the door, armed with my backpack, my notebook and the printouts. Now I know that it was him the other day, I feel more able to confront him. I bang the knocker and, after the second knock, the same guy answers the door.

He looks even less pleased to see me this time. 'You again?'

'You're him aren't you? Detective Frank Firelli?'

He sighs, and then he points his finger at me.

'Your eyesight any good? I've got a bloody splinter.'

'Sure.' I follow him into his kitchen. It's a world of pine. Pine cupboards, benchtop, stools. He hands me some tweezers and a needle. Mum did this for Dad a few times over the years, so I copy what she used to do, and soon I've dug out his splinter. He seems relieved.

'Well then, who are you really?' he snaps, giving me the once-over as he rubs his finger.

'My name is Angus Green. I'm looking into an old case you worked on.'

'Which one?'

'The Robin Winter case. Taskforce Torana.'

He raises a bushy eyebrow. 'Why?'

'It's for an assignment for school.'

'Jesus, that's a blast from the past. Cuppa?'

Soon we're in his lounge room, drinking weak tea. It looks and tastes like he just dipped the cup into a creek. I'm sitting on a worn-out brown leather couch, and he's sitting opposite in an old arm chair, watching me like a hawk. The room is a real man cave. Big TV. Sideboard stocked with booze. Framed rugby poster on the wall. Piles of newspapers by the fire grate. Takeaway containers stacked on the kitchen bench. Everything is dark and run-down, a bit like him. The room smells like wet dog, but oddly I can't see any evidence of one.

'How did you track me down?'

This feels like an interrogation. Once a cop, always a cop?

'Your name is in lots of articles. I googled you and the name of this property came up.'

He makes a grunting noise. 'Bloody internet. Well, you've come to the right place. I led that investigation. But what makes you think you can just rock up here out of nowhere, unannounced, and ask me about my old cases?'

His already furrowed brow is so creased now that he looks like a bloodhound with constipation.

'Like I said, it's a school assignment. I want a good grade.'

'Bullshit. I'd say you're a journalist but you're too young.'

I shake my head. 'I just want to find out more about the case and Robin Winter. I've been researching it.' I take the printouts out of my backpack and hand them to him.

Firelli puts the papers in his lap and flicks through them, periodically peering over his glasses at me. I shift awkwardly on the sofa. His stare is scarily intense. He must have been a tough cop back in the day. I'm glad that Kane and Shell are just outside.

'I'm trying to figure out who kidnapped Robin, and what happened to his mother. What can you tell me about Jane?'

Firelli sits back in his armchair. 'It's not a nice story.'

'I still want to know.' I really do, no matter how tough it might be to hear.

Firelli scratches his chest. 'Jane told me she was originally from a small town called Sarmenal. Her religious parents kicked her out when they found out she was pregnant.'

'Who was Robin's father?'

'She didn't know. Apparently it was a one-night stand. Robin's biological father would have been a logical suspect in the crime, but he would never have known he had a kid. Now, do you want to hear this story or not?'

I bite my tongue and nod.

'She wasn't much older than you are now. Eighteen or nineteen at most. Had guts, coming to a new town, knocked up, with no family or friends. She met some rough types early and ended up selling dope. I'd never come across a pregnant dealer before, and it was a bloody good cover. Took a while for her to get on our radar. She was seeing a guy called Mark Reynolds. He was a really strange bloke, hard to pin down. She told me he was a good man, but they argued a lot over what would happen once the baby came.'

My cuts ache. This might be my real mother he's talking about.

'And she told you all of this herself?'

'Yeah. I got to know her fairly well during the investigation.'

'What was she like, as a person?'

His face softens a bit. 'She was nice enough. Obviously she was hysterical and manic a lot of the time in those early days of the investigation. But there were a couple of times when I managed to speak to her properly. A year or so after the case went cold, the investigation effectively ended, and she disappeared. Never told anyone where she was going, just left.'

'And you don't know where she went?'

'No clue. I think she just wanted to put it all behind her and start again in a new place. I thought she'd stay in touch in case there were any new developments in the case, but I never heard from her again.'

Did the grief make her leave? Or did she just need to get away from Bellanta?

Firelli sighs. 'I can still remember our last conversation. She asked me if I believed in God. She wondered if God had taken her baby away to punish her.'

I'm finding it harder to breathe.

'What did you say?'

'Kid, as a cop, you see such bloody atrocities. The awful things people can do to one another had kicked any idea of God well and truly out of me. I told her she wasn't being punished. That was probably the first time she had ever really smiled since I met her. And that was the last time I saw her.'

'Why not stay in contact with the police? Didn't she want to find Robin?'

'The investigation went on for months, but eventually we hit a wall. So did Jane. I think she was so upset that she had to choose either going under or starting again.'

'What do you reckon happened to her?'

He looks at me intensely. 'Honestly?'

I feel myself bracing my body against the back of the couch.

He leans forward. 'She either made a whole new life for herself, or she fell to bits. Sorry to sound harsh kid, but that's how I see it.'

My legs are shaking.

Firelli gets up out of the chair and I take this as a gesture for me to leave. I have so many questions, but I also want to bawl my eyes out, so I stand up to go.

He eyes me even more intensely, like he's drilling into my brain and rummaging through my memories. He totally knows I've been lying.

'Why are you *really* here?' He's moving closer to me now, eyes still boring into my skull.

I'm terrified. 'I think my Mum was involved somehow,' I blurt out before I even know what I'm doing.

He relaxes a little, smug. He got what he was looking for. And I only have to tell him part of the story.

'Right then. What's your mother's name?'

'Megan Green, but her name before she was married was Megan Cooper.'

'Never heard of her. Why do you think she was involved?'

Should I tell him? I'm not sure what to say.

'Got a picture?' he says before I can answer. 'An old one, preferably from at least ten years ago.'

I scroll through my phone and find the oldest photo of Mum I have. She's at some party with her hair longer and a glass of wine in one hand, mugging for the camera.

'This is her.' I use my fingers to zoom in on Mum's face. He has a close look, lifting his glasses up onto his forehead and holding the phone right up to his eyes. He puts his glasses on again, passing the phone back with an ambiguous look on his face.

Firelli clears his throat. 'I have the old case report and some notes – you want to have a look at them?'

'Really? That would be great.' This is amazing! I've never seen proper case files in real life. How cool to actually see his notes from the actual investigation. Real intel.

'Everything is in the cellar.' He turns and walks to a door that leads into a narrow hallway toward the back of the house. This is going to be great.

'Are you allowed to keep old case reports?' I ask, following him down the dark hallway.

He looks back at me. 'No. But I don't always do the right thing.'

Strange thing to say.

He opens a door at the end of the hall, and flicks a switch. The light barely illuminates the stairs. They seem to disappear into a black hole.

He gestures for me to go. 'After you,' I say feebly. I'm not sure I want to go down there at all, let alone first. A waft of stale, cold air blows through my hair and a sense of dread suddenly washes over me.

He puts a hand on my shoulder. 'No, after you.' I shudder. Suddenly I am falling into darkness.

# Chapter 27

# Cellar

I can hear someone talking to me in the distance. 'Kid? You okay?' I can't make out the voice. My head hurts like crazy. I try to open my eyes but that hurts too. All I know is I'm lying on the floor. It feels cool under me.

'Kid. You slipped on the steps. I tried to grab you. Are you okay?' I remember where I am and realise it's Firelli talking. Did I fall? Or did he push me? Why would he? Unless he took Robin and thinks I'm on to him? I'm starting to panic. I . . . can't . . . breathe . . .

Suddenly Firelli is holding me up. 'Look, you've fallen and had a bit of a shock, but you'll be fine,' he says as he puts his hands under my shoulders. 'Come up just a bit and sit in this chair.' I open my eyes and see genuine concern on his face. Not kidnapper vibes at all. I let him pull me toward the chair and plonk me into it.

We're in a messy, dark cellar with a low ceiling. There's an old roller top desk, a filing cabinet, and a bookcase full of true crime books from what I can tell. There's a heap of junk piled high against one of the walls. Firelli leans against the desk, catching his breath. 'You'll be fine, you're just winded. It's only six steps.'

I feel so embarrassed. And sore.

He rummages around in the filing cabinet by his desk, working his way down the drawers till he finds what he wants. He turns to me with a big folder full of papers secured with blue string.

'I made copies of the case files.'

'Why?'

'If your research is any good, you'll already know that after a couple of weeks, I was taken off the case,' he says, sounding defensive. 'I hadn't made an arrest, and our few suspects had led nowhere. So the Sydney cops moved in and took over, but they made no progress whatsoever.'

There's a flush in his cheeks. 'This was one of those cases you never forget, y'know. I knew who did it, I just couldn't prove it. Being replaced as lead on a local case made me look incompetent. I ended up taking early retirement.' He pats the file in his arms. 'I made copies of key information, determined that one day I would solve it. But I go through this every year with a fine-toothed comb and I still can't find the answers.'

'Can I have a look?'

'Sure.' He puts the folder on the desk and steps aside so I can move my chair over.

There's copies of case notes, photos of Robin and Jane, and of the house and yard. Maps, written statements, forensic reports, newspaper clippings, everything. It's brilliant to see this stuff first hand.

Shell needs to see this. 'Would you mind if I got my friends to join us? They're just outside in the car. We've been investigating this together over the last couple of days.'

Firelli snickers. 'Oh, you've been "investigating" for two whole days have you? What makes you think you can solve something that me and a convoy of Sydney cops couldn't in months, eh?'

I don't know what to say. He's got a point. Firelli shrugs. 'Sure, they can join us. They just can't tell anyone I have these files.'

I text the others and tell them to come straight down to the cellar. I keep flicking through the file until I hear the creak of their feet on the stairs.

Shell nonchalantly surveys the contents of the cellar, then holds out her hand and introduces herself. 'Detective Firelli, I'm Michelle Oliver and this is Kane Parker. We're helping Gus with his cold case investigation.'

Kane raises his hand in a wave.

'"Cold case investigation"! Ha! You kids are a hoot.'

'Guys, come check this out,' I say, holding up the files. They start to look through the contents with me, their eyes widening.

'Wow, these are so interesting.' Shell flicks through a few of the pages. 'But does this bring us any closer to who did it?'

Kane hands the folder back to me.

'You kids never saw this, got it?' Firelli says, wagging his finger.

We nod.

'You said you knew who did it. Who?' I ask.

Firelli grunts. 'Mark Reynolds, without a doubt. Jane wouldn't stop dealing, and he was angry, and afraid that Robin would be taken off her. He had a record for theft, had been in and out of foster care. Plus he was just strange in interviews. I knew he was lying. Problem was his alibi – it was rock-solid. Too many people saw him at the pub that afternoon. I kept surveillance on him for weeks, blew my budget hoping that we could figure out how he did it and where he was keeping Robin – but we got nothing.'

'Why were you so sure it was him and not one of the other suspects?'

Firelli shakes his head. 'In these cases, you *always* look at the family first. Jane had no motive that we could find. Her family had effectively disowned her, but we interviewed them and cleared them. Besides Jane and Robin, three other people visited the house that day, all at around the same time, so they were all suspects by default. Jane had a daily nap at 3 pm, and two of them knew her well enough to know her routine. But there was just no clear motive or any evidence linking any of them to his disappearance. I had them all watched too, just in case, but none of them did anything suspicious.'

He starts pacing around the room, which is tricky given how small it is. Periodically he stops and fiddles with his de-splintered finger. 'Beyond those three, we trawled through Jane's customers, past and present, but came up with nothing. No customers seemed to have a grudge against her, and she was paid up with her suppliers. Our hope was that we would find Robin eventually. We ran volunteer search parties, door-to-door searches, the lot, but still nothing turned up.'

'But you're sure it was Mark, not just some random who saw Robin in the yard and took him?'

'Yes.' His voice is steely. He's clearly still angry about this. 'I've always been convinced it was Reynolds. Interviewing him that first time, there was something in his eyes. I've been a cop most of my life and I *know* when someone is lying.'

'If Mark was never charged, how did the media get his name?' I ask.

Firelli sighs. 'One of the team let it slip somewhere. We were all convinced he did it, but his name should have been protected.'

'Look, I don't want to be rude, especially since you're a detective,' says Shell carefully. 'But is there *any* chance you were so sure he did it that you missed something back then?'

His face flashes, annoyed, his mouth open as though he's about to yell at her. Suddenly he sighs and his demeanour changes. 'I've gone back over the case many times over the years and I still can't find enough motive, opportunity, let alone evidence to point to anyone else.'

'We've been interviewing people for the last couple of days. Maybe we found something new, something that didn't come out at the time?' I say hopefully.

Firelli rolls his eyes and scoffs.

'It can't hurt to hear us out, can it?' Kane says.

'Sure kid, I guess it can't hurt.' He spreads out our printouts and looks at my notes from the last two days.

I kick things off. 'Okay, so first we spoke to old Mrs Crale who lives directly over the road from Jane's house.'

Firelli looks surprised. 'Still alive, is she? We spoke to her and her husband back in the day. She said she saw the other three that day, but didn't see Reynolds. Mind you, she was scatterbrained back then, didn't make a lot of sense. On a lot of medication, apparently.'

She mentioned medication the other day, too. I continue. 'She thought it might have been Dr Christow.'

Firelli clasps his hands together. 'He was a smug bastard, but I could never see Jane's rejection of him as a real motive. And he had too much to lose, like his career and standing in the community. Plus he's still in town, so what did he do with the kid?'

Shell and I exchange a look and move on, not dwelling on the implications.

'We spoke to him too, briefly. He suggested it might be Sophie Baxter.'

Firelli rubs his de-splintered finger across his chin. 'Interesting, but again there's the question of what she did with him.'

I mention Anna and Firelli immediately rolls his eyes.

'I did wonder about her. She seemed unhinged enough to use a kidnapped child to prove her powers. But he would have been able to identify her when we found him, and there wasn't anything in it for her to keep him.'

Kane laughs. 'Maybe she wore a mask, like in *Scream*?'

'This isn't a joke, mate,' Firelli says. Kane folds his arms defensively.

Firelli turns back to the papers on the desk. 'I did wonder if Jane may have done it, but I could never see a decent motive, unless she had accidentally killed the kid and wanted to cover it up. But it didn't make sense with her reaction or behaviour after he went missing.'

While Firelli talks, Kane is going through the files. Suddenly he stops at the back of the folder, and inhales sharply. 'Um, who exactly is this?' He holds up a photo to Firelli. I can't see it from where I'm sitting.

'What do you mean? That's Mark Reynolds.'

Kane is white in the face. 'Gus, you *gotta* see this.'

Eagerly, I take the photocopied page from him. What's the big deal?

'No. It can't be . . .' My hand is shaking. 'This is my dad!'

*Chapter 28*

# Photo

'Christ on a bike!' Firelli shouts, staring at me. His eyes are bright and alert. 'Mark Reynolds called himself your father? Does that make you Robin?' He grabs my chin and examines my face really closely. 'You could be, you know, now that I look at the shape of your face properly.'

I feel sick, deep in the pit of my stomach. I want to run outside and scream and hide in my cubbyhouse. I don't know what to say so I just nod. I can't really believe it, I know I've been suspecting the truth all this time.

Shell is hugging me, Kane has his hands on my shoulders, and I can feel tears on my face. Until now it had never felt *real*. But the truth is right in front of me now, undeniable. I don't know what I feel. Tired, mostly. Very tired.

I wanted this. I wanted answers. But I didn't know it would feel like this.

'I knew he did it!' Firelli yells, fuelled by righteous justification. Suddenly the air seems different in the room, electric somehow. The expression on Firelli's face changes from excited to angry to pensive in turns. I guess there's a lot of feelings coming back for him too.

He turns to me. 'Does your mother know who Reynolds is?'

*What did she know?*

'I don't know,' I show him the printout from the website that

185

started all of this. 'When I showed her this picture, she wouldn't tell me anything. I got a DNA test done, which proves we aren't biologically related. When I confronted her, she just said I was adopted. But she must have known.'

'And Reynolds is still pretending to be your father?'

I shake my head. 'No, he died five years ago.'

He looks a bit deflated. 'Damn, would have liked to confront that bastard. How did he die? Foul play?'

This is tough, hearing him talk about Dad like he was a criminal. 'Car accident.'

Firelli sits back down, staring intensely at nothing. There's silence for a bit. I rub my eyes. I can't quite take all of this in.

'Why do you think he did it?' Shell asks.

'Look, he was a bloody strange bloke, capable of anything. Jane told me that they argued a lot, because Reynolds was worried Robin would be taken away from her if Community Services found out about her dealing. She said he'd had a rough childhood in foster care, and so he probably convinced himself that he was saving Robin by taking him.'

I am trying to wrap my head around this. My cuts are on fire. 'So that picture I showed you of Mum – she wasn't ever involved in this?'

'Not that I know of, no.'

I'm feeling guilty now after what I accused Mum of. But while she may not have been technically involved, she can't be completely innocent either.

Firelli starts pacing the room. 'So, Reynolds took you and hid you away. But where? We pulled this damn town apart looking for you.'

I wish he would stop looking at me like I have answers. 'I don't remember anything before late 2010.'

'That's around when the main investigation started to ease off.

We had no reason to keep track of him by then. I simply could not break his alibi.'

'Why was his alibi so solid?' I ask.

'He was at the pub drinking all day. There's security footage has him there from 2.00 pm until 7.00 pm, when the barman kicked him out because he was so drunk. That was two hours after Jane had reported Robin missing. Everyone at the bar insisted he never left.'

I shake my head, frowning. 'Then who took me? How did I end up in Melbourne? It doesn't make any sense.'

'I don't know, kid. He couldn't have slipped out to take you without anyone noticing. Believe me, I tested it myself. It's a forty-minute round trip from the pub to the house and back again. Once you add the time it would take to grab and hide a child, it would have taken an hour or more. Even if he drove, I don't see how he could have done it.'

Firelli is staring at me thoughtfully. 'But today, you are telling me that you were raised by Mark Reynolds, posing as your father. So the fact is he *was* involved, but he must have gotten someone else to actually take you. This changes *everything*.'

'Who would have helped him?' asks Shell.

Firelli starts to count on his fingers. 'Well that takes us back to those other three suspects. If one of them was just an accomplice, it would explain why we struggled to pin a motive on any of them.'

'Didn't you look into all of this back then?' asks Kane.

Firelli glares at him, clearly unhappy having his investigation questioned. He visibly grits his teeth. 'Of course we did. But we were looking at connections to Jane and Robin, not specific connections to Reynolds. When we couldn't break his alibi, and no new evidence emerged, we had to shift our focus.'

He turns to me, pointing at the aged-up picture of Robin – of me – that we brought. 'But now we *know* that Reynolds did it, and we *know* he must have had an accomplice, so now we can re-interview the other three suspects.' He's breathing heavily as he paces the room. Another chance to solve his unsolved case.

'We should start with Mrs Crale,' I say. 'Yesterday she started to tell me about someone who wasn't in the yard that day, but we got interrupted.'

He stops pacing and stares into space. 'What does that mean?' He drums his fingers on top of the filing cabinet, talking to himself. 'It all makes sense now. Someone was helping him – not just for the kidnapping but for the weeks and months that followed. You can't just take a kid and hide them while you're the number one suspect. Even once things quietened down, in this century you can't just up and start a new life under a new name without a paper trail. He'd need a birth certificate at least.'

Shell is pacing the room now, like Firelli was earlier. 'So, Mark took him, with help from someone, and left town with him after things died down. But when he hooked up with Gus's mum in Melbourne, what did he tell her? She must know something about this.'

I shake my head. 'Unless Mum met Dad later, when he was passing me off as his kid. Maybe that's why she told me I was adopted the other day? Maybe that's what she was told?'

'We'll have to report this,' Firelli says, crossing his arms. 'This is a serious breakthrough.'

'What happens if Mum did know?' I ask.

Firelli looks at me, grey sadness in his eyes. 'Kidnappers usually get ten plus years, but it sounds like she'd be an accessory after the fact. That's fairly minor compared to the kidnapping itself. If she made a full admission then she might be charged, but put on a good behaviour bond.'

'I don't know what to do now,' I say. I really don't. I feel like I don't know anything anymore, except that I want to make this feeling go away. I want to cut, to control all these feelings.

'Well, okay. I need to be clear with you, kid. Assuming this is all true – remembering we have no hard evidence yet – and you are Robin Winter, here's what happens next. First, those other suspects need to be interviewed again. Second, we need to speak to your mother and determine how much she knew.'

'What if we just don't tell police?' Shell asks.

'You've told me now, and I can't sit with this. Knowing I was right isn't enough. This is a major crime.'

I scratch my birthmarks furiously. Firelli must see I'm falling to bits here. He rest his hand on my shoulder. 'I won't report this *just* yet. We still don't have the full picture,' he pauses. 'Hey, how old are you?'

'Fifteen. Sixteen in a few weeks.'

'Still a minor. If she gets a good behaviour bond, you may be put into care until you're eighteen.'

'What?'

In all of this it never crossed my mind that I'm legally a child. Sergeant East mentioned it the other day, but I didn't really take any notice at the time.

'You've opened a can of worms here that you can't just shut I'm afraid, kid,' Firelli says.

'I need to know the truth, whatever happens,' I say, almost trying to convince myself.

Kane has been quiet through most of this. 'Someone else out there wants to know the truth too,' he says gently.

It feels like forever since I found the website. 'Do you think Jane put the post online? Maybe she's still alive and out there somewhere?'

Firelli shrugs. 'Maybe. But it could be anyone.'

Kane says what I've been thinking. 'Why not just ask your mum?'

'Why don't you just text her?' I bark back. Immediately I regret it, and try to calm myself down before continuing. 'Sorry. I just don't think I'll get the truth out of her till we know the full story.'

Firelli makes a move toward the stairs. Suddenly Shell claps her hands together in triumph.

'I know what we need to do. A sting operation! Get 'em all in one place face-to-face, see if you can catch one of them out.'

Firelli shakes his head in exasperation. 'Bloody hell, you kids are crazy. This isn't a video game or a bloody TV show. That's not how these things work at all. A senior detective would never do that, especially without any hard evidence.'

I smile. 'But *you* could do it.'

Firelli raises an eyebrow. 'Eh?'

'Well, you've retired, so you don't *have* to act like a senior detective anymore. You could just ask them to come to Jane's house to answer some questions.'

He crosses his arms. 'That's ridiculous.'

'Is it?' Kane says. 'You know more now that you did back then, and putting them on the spot could make one of them slip up.' Kane taps his chin, thoughtful. 'Even if one of them only *helped* kidnap Gus, they could still be dangerous.'

I never thought of that.

Shell stares at Firelli. I know this look. She has an idea and she's going to talk him into it – he just doesn't know it yet.

'One of these three people has been covering up a crime for years, but now you have a sure-fire way to shake them into confessing.'

Firelli smirks and folds his arms across his chest. 'Hmmph. And what might that be? There's no evidence!'

Shell points at me. 'You have the victim! Invite them all to the house where it all started, and introduce Gus as Robin. It'll be such a shock to one of them that they may give themselves away,' she claps her hands together. 'Ta-dah! You have your accomplice.'

Firelli stares at her. Then me. Back to her.

'Utterly ridiculous . . .'

Shell grins at him. 'You'll get to solve a cold case. You can restore your reputation.'

His face shifts and a germ of a smile appears.

Kane is less enthusiastic. 'Sounds dangerous to me. What do you think Gus?'

I don't know what to think. It could be a way to get the last pieces of the puzzle together.

'Dunno. Might work,' I mutter.

Firelli opens the bottom drawer of the filing cabinet and grabs a bottle of whiskey and a glass out of it. He pours a decent shot for himself, then downs it in one gulp. 'I must be going senile but I reckon this might just work,' he smiles at me. 'But only if you want to do it.'

I can feel Shell's excitement and concern at the same time, like sun on a rainy day. 'You definitely don't have to do this,' she says.

Kane comes over, resting his hand on my forearm. 'No Goose, you don't.'

'Buuuut,' she adds, 'if you do, we'll all be right there with you.'

I'm so close to answers that I feel like I can almost touch them. I take a deep breath. 'Okay. Let's do this.'

'I'll invite them over to Mather Street tomorrow. They'll all remember me.'

Kane scratches his head. 'What if they don't want to come?'

Firelli cracks his knuckles. 'I'll explain that we have a breakthrough in the case. They'll come out of sheer curiosity, if nothing else.'

My head is bursting and the fishhooks are back. I can't get my head around Dad being Mark, one of the people we've met being his accomplice, setting a trap for them.

'Ok, here's Anna's number. Kane's got Sophie's. Christow's should be easy enough to get.' Shell grabs some paper and a pen from Firelli's desk and writes down the numbers.

'Thanks kid,' he tucks the paper into his pocket. 'Alright, go get some rest. We'll talk in the morning.'

And just like that I am suddenly a decoy in some off-the-books sting operation. A few days ago this would have been the most exciting thing ever. But now I'm just worried.

* * *

Everyone is drained from the day, so we end up eating dinner at Foxy's again.

'I'm sorry I didn't ask you first before saying we should use you for bait with the suspects. It just came to me in a flash.' Shell squeezes my hand.

'It's a good idea, I just . . .' I don't know what to say. Or feel or think.

Kane gives me a reassuring smile. 'You need a good sleep if you're gonna be kidnapper bait, Goose.'

We all go to bed early.

Later, when I can hear Shell and Kane snoring, I sneak outside. The night sky is so clear in the country. I swear there are literally hundreds more stars out here than I've ever seen in Melbourne. They remind me of the time Dad put stick-on glow-in-the-dark stars on my bedroom ceiling one year when I was a kid. Like most DIY things he did, it didn't quite work. The stars didn't stick properly and several fell onto my bed and the floor over the next few days. One fell on my face in the middle of the night, scaring me half to death. Could that kind, clumsy, peppercorn-dust man really be my kidnapper?

I shiver. It's not that cold, but I'm shit-scared about tomorrow. Scared of what might happen if I do this, but scared that I'll never know the truth if I don't. Either way, I feel like my old life is disappearing, like breath on a mirror.

# Chapter 29

# Sting

I sleep badly. There's a universe in my head full of dark dreams, about Dad, about my life not being mine, and being trapped in a cellar. The dreams bounce around like satellites in deep space, forming black holes inside me, where time folds in on itself.

Firelli has already texted saying that Christow, Sophie and Anna will all be at Mather Street at 10 am. I guess I would come too, no matter how odd this 'new evidence' story seemed.

Funny to think of myself as evidence.

Once we arrive, Firelli checks that I'm still okay to do this. I tell him yes, I am. He positions me at the side of the house, hidden behind one of the worn-out trellises. From here, I can see and hear everything that happens out front. Kane is next to me, getting ready to film it all through one of the gaps in the trellis.

Firelli is by the front gate, clean shaven, his hair slicked back. He stands with his feet apart, hands crossed over his chest. His shirt, aviator jacket, and trousers are all dark blue. From a distance, he looks like he's in uniform. Shell is standing with him, same stance, ready to give me the signal when the time comes. Both of them look like they mean business.

Sophie is the first to arrive, getting out of an old yellow Toyota Corolla. She looks upset. 'Detective Sergeant Firelli. What is this new evidence?'

He looks her up and down. 'I'll let you know soon, Ms Baxter. I'm just waiting for two other people to arrive. Perhaps you'd like to take a seat on the fence?'

She seems a little miffed by this but sits down and starts fiddling on her phone, her left foot nervously tapping.

I barely have time to analyse her reaction before Christow's black Lexus pulls up. He still looks intimidating, and pissed off. He marches straight up to Firelli. 'I don't see why you couldn't have told us what's going on over the phone. I have a full list today and I don't like palming patients off to my colleague.'

Christow stands very close to him, trying to intimidate him. They are the same height, but Firelli doesn't flinch. 'Please wait with Ms Baxter, Dr Christow. We have one more person coming.' Firelli calmly gestures toward the fence.

Only then does Christow seem to notice Sophie sitting nearby. She has been looking at him since he arrived, eyes wary like a cat, her foot tapping overtime now.

He ignores her, lighting up a smoke and jingling his car keys impatiently. She sneers at him.

There's silence for a few minutes, then Anna arrives on a rusty old bike. She screeches to a stop and swings her legs dramatically to dismount. She stops in her tracks when she sees Sophie and Christow.

'Well, this is a surprise,' she says as she walks past them and up to Firelli.

'Really?' Sophie scoffs. 'I thought you would have predicted this whole event.'

'Lovely to see you again too,' Anna says evenly. Then she turns to Firelli. 'What's all this?'

'Yes, tell us about this new evidence,' snarls Christow. 'Some of us are busy.'

Firelli nods curtly, and uncrosses his arms. 'Right. Thank you all for coming. I asked you all here today as each of you were persons of interest in the case of Robin Winter.'

Sophie shifts uncomfortably on the fence.

'As I said on the phone last night, new evidence has come to light recently. You may remember that our prime suspect was Mark Reynolds. I can now confirm that he did indeed take Robin.'

For a second there is no reaction, but then they all start speaking at once.

Christow snorts. 'So we're cleared. Can we go now?'

'What?' cries Sophie.

Anna tilts her head to one side. 'Yes, but why are we here?'

Kane zooms his camera in on each of their faces.

Shell gives me the signal as Firelli continues. 'Mark Reynolds did take Robin. He took him down to Victoria, changed his name to Angus Green, and raised him as his own son.'

I step out from behind the trellis into the yard. All eyes on me. It feels so weird, like stepping onto a stage without knowing my lines. I can feel my face going bright red.

'This is Robin Winter, all grown up,' says Firelli.

Everyone reacts at the same time. Christow snarls, possibly at me, possibly at Firelli, and drags deeply on his cigarette, exhaling smoke out of his nostrils like a bull. Sophie's eyes widen and she makes a small choking noise, her hand covering her mouth in shock. Anna jumps to her feet, eyes ablaze. 'I *knew* I felt something yesterday when you visited!'

Firelli smiles evenly at them all. 'We now believe that Reynolds had an accomplice who actually took Robin on the day, and then helped hide him during the investigation.'

Firelli pauses for a moment to let this sink in.

'And you think it was one of us?' Anna says.

Firelli nods. 'I do.'

Christow throws his hands up in frustration, 'I'm glad to see that Robin wasn't killed, but how does this prove any of us were involved? It could have been anyone.' He looks me directly in the eye. 'Don't you remember who took you that day?'

I stare at my feet. 'No. I wish I did.'

Christow turns back to Firelli, triumphant, 'So, *detective*, nothing's really changed, has it? Go and arrest Reynolds and leave us in peace.'

While Christow is going off at Firelli, Sophie has been staring at me. She gets to her feet. 'Robin? Is it really you?'

I can't say the words, it's all too new. I nod.

She holds her arms out to me. I think she expects me to come to her, but I'm not doing that. When I don't, she steps closer. Thankfully, Shell steps in, blocking her like a bodyguard.

'I don't think that's a good idea right now.'

Sophie glares at her, but seems to realise she's right, and steps away again.

Anna shakes her head at Sophie. 'I see you're still obsessed.'

'I haven't seen him for years. It's concern, not obsession.'

Anna turns to Firelli. 'Perhaps if you had listened to me back in the day, Robin could have been found years ago. You wrote me off as a fraud without ever giving me a chance.'

Firelli looks a little flustered, but keeps his composure. 'We looked everywhere. You said you felt he was under a house, so we searched every cellar and basement in town and the surrounds.'

Sophie points at Christow. 'He's got a basement, did you check there? Jane said he kept fancy wine down there.'

Christow is furious. 'Shut up!' he yells at Sophie.

'Stop!' yells Firelli.

Sophie looks both shocked and somehow also pleased he's shown his true colours.

'We found no trace of Robin at his house, or yours for that matter,' says Firelli.

Shell looks at Sophie and Anna. 'Both of you thought the doctor here did it. Why were you so sure?'

Sophie glares at Christow. 'He's a nasty piece of work. Jane was scared of him.'

Anna nods. 'You don't have to be gifted to see that he is violent.'

'Stop it, the lot of you!' yells Firelli. 'This ends today. One of you helped Mark Reynolds and I want to know who. Now!'

None of them say anything.

'Where's your evidence?' Christow says smugly.

All eyes are on Firelli now.

He coughs, clearing his throat. 'Mark Reynolds posed as Angus's – Robin's – father. Gus is the evidence.'

All three of them are bickering. Firelli is starting to lose his cool. Shell steps in and tells them to settle down, like she's a teacher herding children.

That's when I notice Mrs Crale over the road, hunched over a rose bush in her garden, watching this all unfold.

I nudge Shell. 'Mrs Crale is watching. I wanna ask her again about what she meant to say last time. Seeing them all here might have sparked her memory.'

Shell nods and takes my notebook.

'Let's go through your alibis again, one by one . . .' says Firelli. Shell starts scribbling as the three of them start talking. I make my way across the road.

Mrs Crale sees me coming towards her and waves, secateurs in her hand. If she was just spying, rather than pruning, she sure has the right prop.

'Hi Mrs Crale. It's Angus.'

'Yes, I remember dear.' She looks unsteady, but her cheeks are rosy.

'The police are talking with the three people you said visited the house the day Robin was taken.'

She looks sheepishly at me. 'Yes.'

'Have you remembered anything else about that day?'

'Oh yes,' she nods enthusiastically.

'Such as?' *Give me something here!*

She stares into the distance. 'What's that, dear?'

*Sheesh.* 'The police now know that Mark Reynolds took Robin.'

'Mark? No,' she shakes her head.

'The police think he had an accomplice who physically took Robin for him that day. They think it's one of these three people.'

'I see.'

'The other day, you said that there was someone that you *didn't* see in the yard that day.'

She's confused. 'Sorry?'

'Did you see one of those people actually take Robin that day?'

Blinking, she seems to snap back to reality. 'Do you want a cup of tea? I find a nice cuppa helps me think more clearly, don't you?'

At this point I'll say yes to anything if it means getting answers.

She unlatches the front door and walks down the hall slowly. I follow her, noting the rose-themed wallpaper on the walls, faded but still intact. Everything is clean and tidy. She leads me to an old-fashioned kitchen. A row of china plates decorate the mantelpiece over the stove, also patterned with roses.

I'm pleased to see Mr Crale isn't here.

She flicks the kettle on and spoons in some tea leaves from a tin container into a china teapot. Sitting at the kitchen table, I notice a medical needle sitting on a plate by the sugar bowl. Weird.

Mrs Crale puts the steaming teapot on the table with two cups.

'That's my morphine shot dear. I have stage four breast cancer. It helps with the pain,' she says, as if it's as ordinary as saying she has a runny nose.

'I'm sorry to hear that.'

'All my years nursing made me accept that death is just another stage of life. Now, tea.'

'Mrs Crale, what did you see in Robin's yard that day?'

She fingers an ugly cameo brooch pinned to the collar of her cardigan. 'I saw Robin in the front yard, trying to eat two-minute noodles, dry from the packet. It broke my heart. Do you want a biscuit?' she asks, leaning over the table to my right.

As I go to take one, I feel a strange stab in my arm.

'Ouch!'

'Sorry dear, I scratched you with my brooch.' She holds the cameo brooch in her hand, the clasp open.

'It's okay. Can you tell me about that day please?' I feel a bit lightheaded.

'Oh, do you want to see my garden? Many more roses there.'

She takes my arm and slowly leads me out the back door and down the steps. I go to text Shell but realise I have left my phone on the kitchen table.

She takes me around the side of the house. We stop in front of two big glass doors that look like they lead to a cellar. She opens the doors and gently guides me downstairs. It's semi-dark in here, but there is quite a bit of light coming from a skylight. She turns on an internal light.

It's a decent-sized cellar. There is a huge table, a couple of chairs, and a tall bookcase full of gardening gear.

'Aren't they lovely?' she asks, pointing to row upon row of rose seedlings and cuttings in pots on the table. I can't seem to focus properly. My mind is foggy.

'I breed them in my greenhouse . . . well, I call it that, but it's really a cellar. Bill put in some skylights, see?' She points to the ceiling. 'Let me show you how I breed my roses. First you choose the parents, then you prepare the mother by removing all the petals and then the stamen, so that it can't self-pollinate.'

I feel properly drowsy. *What's happening to me?*

'My roses are my legacy. Bill and I were not blessed with children of our own. That's why we fostered Mark.'

'Mark Reynolds?' I hear myself ask, but as if from a long way away.

I'm so woozy now I can barely stand. She guides me to a chair and I fall into it.

'Sit, dear.' She leans in close to me, stroking my face with her bony old lady hands as I drift into sleep. 'You're safe now, Robin.'

# Chapter 30

# Burns

When I wake up I can't breathe properly. It feels like everything is caving in on me. Like I'm being crushed, my old life disappearing, erased. Angus Green is no longer a person. Just a dream someone once had.

Mrs Crale is muttering away nearby. 'You needed a good feed. Mark and I agreed that if nothing else, he would always keep you well-fed.'

Suddenly there is another shape blocking the light. Standing in the doorway is Mr Crale.

'What have you done Esther?' he yells. She is cowering in the corner, looking sheepish.

'It's him, after all these years. He's come back to me.'

Mr Crale comes closer and has a good look at me. 'So it *is* you,' he says. I'm momentarily blinded by the sudden change in light. I can't tell if he's angry or surprised or something else entirely.

'Esther said it was you, but I wasn't sure.'

'You kept me here?' My head is groggy. I reach for my phone, but it's not there. I remember I left it inside.

Mrs Crale is smiling at me, a strange, kooky smile. 'I'd remember the shape of your face anywhere. And when you showed me that photo of Mark and that woman, I knew.'

I can't take all of this in. I try to get up but I'm too dizzy.

'What have you done to me?'

'I'm sorry dear, I gave you a shot of my morphine. It is very strong.'

I rub my arm. Clearly it wasn't the brooch that pricked me. 'Why?'

'I need to keep you safe. I can protect you from her.'

'Her?' For a minute I think she means Mum, but then I realise she means Jane.

She starts rambling in a strange sing-song voice, her tiny body swaying. 'She wasn't feeding you properly. You were so skinny, like a string bean. And you were being hurt.'

'Stop this now, Esther,' snaps Mr Crale. His face is red.

But she keeps going, talking to me. 'You wandered over to our house one day. You looked so scrawny I gave you some soup and you spilled some on your shirt. I went to clean you up and saw the marks on your arms. Cigarette burns. Fresh. As a nurse I knew them instantly.'

I clumsily roll up my right sleeve to look at what I always thought were just two birthmarks. They burn when I touch them. *All this time . . .* I shudder.

'You wandered over here again the next day for food. And the day after that. I was worried for your safety. Mark was furious when I told him. So we made a plan.'

I'm trying to join the dots logically in my head but my brain is too foggy. I want to scream but I'm struggling to even speak properly.

'But I don't . . . remember . . . you at all.'

'You were young dear, you've probably blanked it out. Children have the most resilient minds sometimes.' She keeps swaying, smiling to herself. 'Mark was so clever. He got me to get the doctor and the babysitter over by pretending to be Jane on the phone, after I'd already taken you. He wanted to give the police some suspects, and he knew she'd be sleeping. She wouldn't answer her phone or the door.'

I can't believe all this happened to me and I'm stuck here in this weird cellar finding out the truth, drugged, slurring my words.

'But . . . you said "they" weren't there . . . who did you mean?'

'Your terrible mother! *She* wasn't there. You should never have been in that yard on your own,' she snaps. Then she smiles. 'Mark and I planned it all without telling Bill.'

I put my hand on my throbbing forehead. 'Why didn't you just call . . . social services? Or the police? Why this?'

Mrs Crale shakes her head. 'We couldn't do that. You would have been taken into foster care. Mark grew up in awful care homes and . . . well, we couldn't let that happen.'

I stare at the Crales standing there together. Her looking unhinged. Him looking at her, concerned and confused.

'We did it for your safety,' she says. 'It was all for you, Robin.'

'But you . . . you took me from my mother. I was . . . just a little kid.' What must Jane have felt? Sophie said that it broke her. Firelli said she felt punished by God.

I rub my eyes furiously as a tear rolls down my face.

Mrs Crale leans forward, reaching out to me. 'Don't cry Robin, we did the right thing.'

And that's when I make my move. I push her away and make a dash for the door. Mr Crale goes to catch her, as expected, so I manage to get past him too and scramble up the stairs. Her wig slips awry as she stumbles, revealing a pale, mainly bald head, with just a few grey wisps of hair. I turn and keep going but almost fall over when I get outside into the glaring light. The morphine is still slowing me down.

Outside I try to get round to the front to alert Shell and Kane and Firelli. 'Shell! Kane!' I stumble and fall. When I get up again, Mr Crale is blocking my way to the path around the side of the house. With nowhere else to go, I run to the back of their yard, nearly tripping over the garden hose as I go. Mr Crale is chasing me, albeit slowly.

The back fence is too high to climb over. I'm trapped and he's still coming for me. I spot a loose paling on the fence to my right. Desperately, I pull it free and try to squeeze through, but I get stuck halfway.

'Robiiiin, do you want some noodles?' Mrs Crale creepy sing-song voice sounds completely nuts now. Mr Crale's almost on me. I breathe in deep and push myself through the fence, falling to the ground on the other side. Mr Crale is a big unit too, so he's struggling to get through after me. It gives me a few seconds to get to my feet and keep running. But there's nowhere to go except back into someone else's yard.

Then I see the creek.

Maybe if I can just get across it I can lose him and loop back around to find the others?

I stumble over to the edge of the creek. It looks deep, but it's only about ten metres wide. I know I can make it. I look back. He's through the fence now and running after me. His face is red with anger and exertion. I reckon Mr Crale's swimming days are behind him.

I step over the railing and jump into the creek. It's darker and colder than I expected. I sink deep and swallow a fair bit of water before I come up for air, gasping and spluttering.

I can't breathe. I start to panic. Need a breath. Gulping. The drugs must be really kicking in. I can barely keep my head up. I'm thrashing about, getting nowhere. My eyes are heavy. The creek is pulling me down.

Deeper. Deeper.

Blackness as I slide under.

# Chapter 31

# Creek

Someone is pulling me up. My head is yanked above water, and suddenly I can breathe. I'm spluttering out water, then gulping down air. More air.

Kane has me, holding my chin up, guiding me back to the bank. I don't understand what's happened at first. I let his strength support me, drag me along. All I seem to have the energy for is breathing.

He pulls me out of the water and onto the bank. I flop back, shirt ridden up, showing my scars. He pulls my shirt down and grabs my shoulder. 'Goose, you okay?'

'Gus!' Shell's breathless voice is nearby.

I shake my head like a wet dog, wheezing still.

Shell has Mr Crale on the ground, arm twisted behind his back, holding him down. Firelli is holding Mrs Crale's hand, like she's a child. In her other hand is her wig, clutched to her chest like a precious fluffy toy.

I think Kane has just saved my life. 'Since when can you swim?'

He grins. 'Your mum has been teaching me, using the pool at physio. That's the favour I mentioned.'

'Right. Well, um, thanks for saving my life.'

'Now we're even.'

I sit up properly, taking in what's been happening around me. 'Nice tackle, Shell,' Kane says. She looks fierce.

Firelli finishes reading them their rights, still holding Mrs Crale's hand. She looks so frail and confused. He's all fired up, yelling. 'You helped Mark kidnap and hide that boy!'

Mrs Crale nods like an eager child. 'Yes. We kept him safe.'

'For months?'

She nods again. 'Yes. Safe. Kept him safe.' She keeps repeating it to herself, a quiet mantra.

'You're both coming to the station with me, *now*.'

Shell releases Mr Crale and drags him to his feet. Firelli takes his arm too.

I sit up and shiver. Shell rushes over to me and hugs me.

Suddenly Mrs Crale fixes her eyes on me, lucid for a moment. 'Is Mark well? Is he a good father to you?'

'You didn't stay in touch?' I ask.

'No, we agreed no contact was safer. Safe . . .' She really has lost it.

'He's dead,' I say softly.

She lets out a wail like a wounded animal. I've never heard anything like it. Mr Crale and Firelli catch her together and try to hold her up as she sobs and crumples, like a flower folding in on itself.

'How?' Mr Crale asks.

'Car accident . . . about five years ago.'

His eyes water. 'Was it quick?'

'Yes,' I lie.

Mr Crale shakes his head. 'He wasn't a bad person you know. He cared for you. So did Esther.'

I can't believe I'm feeling bad for the people who took me from Jane all those years ago, but I do. And I also feel super tired. Might be the morphine. Might just be everything.

Kane stands up now, arms crossed, an angry look on his face, water dripping from his hair.

'Is one of you gonna apologise for what you did to Gus? You pinched him and kept him from his mother. You're sick,' he barks.

Shell's fired up too, full-force death staring them. 'Did you stand by the window and watch his mum falling apart over the road every day while you held her child hostage?'

Firelli is shaking his head in disgust. 'And you lied to investigators every day. We searched your home. Where did you hide him?'

Mr Crale is cupping his wife's bald head as she quietly sobs. 'After the first night, I partitioned off the room a little and hid the door with that bookcase. I was a carpenter by trade so it was easy to do.' He looks over at me, guilt in his eyes. 'We only put you there when the police were around. It was well ventilated. And you were always quiet if you had your two-minute noodles. The rest of the time you could run around the cellar, which you seemed to like.'

I try to get up, swaying a bit, still unsteady on my feet. Shell glares at the Crales and grabs my arm.

'Let me help.'

Kane takes my other arm and together they haul me up. I'm dripping wet and exhausted, but I feel like a hundred weights have been lifted from my chest.

'What have you done with the other suspects?' I ask Firelli, shaking water out of one ear, then the other, and then holding my nose and blowing to pop them.

Firelli grins. 'I left them there when we came looking for you. I'll let them know they're off the hook now. You did a good job, kid,' Firelli says as he guides the Crales away. 'I'm sorry that we weren't able to help you back then. But I'm glad to be here now to finish the job at least.'

I don't know what to say, I just stutter out a thanks.

'Go home kid, talk to your mother. Find out what she knew. Then give me a bell. I won't say anything about her until I've heard from you.'

I nod, splutter out some more creek water, and start to cry. Huge, hot tears. Crying for everything and nothing and all the things in between.

# Chapter 32

# Confession

We drive back to the motel, me wrapped in a picnic blanket from the boot, dripping water over Kane's vinyl car seats. I have a long, hot shower. Standing under the water, I feel exhausted and invigorated at the same time. It feels good to wash away the tears and the taste of the creek. I just stand there till the water runs cold. When it's Kane's turn, he tells me off for using all the hot water.

When we've finally rinsed the creek off, we bundle up all our stuff and start the four-hour drive back to Melbourne. Just before I nod off, I finally text Mum.

*On my way home. We need to talk about Mark Reynolds.*

*Yes Gussy, we do. I've missed you so much.*

The last thing I see before I go to sleep is the 'Goodbye, thank you for visiting Bellanta' sign. As it fades away behind us, I feel like maybe part of my childhood has too. Images of Mum and Dad bounce around my head. How can the nice tall man with the big smile who let me ride the lawnmower be a kidnapper?

I wake up as we hit the freeway into Melbourne. My neck is stiff from my head being slumped on the window. Kane drops Shell off first.

I stand with her as she lugs her suitcase out of the boot of the car. Plonking it down in front of her, she smiles softly at me. 'You okay? What are you going to say to her?'

'Dunno. Won't know till it comes out my mouth. It feels so weird. What about you? Are you gonna talk to your parents?'

She runs her hands over her head. 'Yeah. The last few days have stirred up some courage in me, finally.'

'Well you helped solve a crime and tackled a kidnapper to the ground. Impressive stuff.'

'All in a day's work, Gus.'

She reaches over and gently kisses my cheek. 'Good luck. Text me, whatever happens, yeah?'

'Same with you. They love you. It'll work out okay.'

I know it's cringey, but I feel like I'm saying my last goodbye to her as Gus. I'm not sure who I will be the next time I see her. Who either of us will be.

'Good luck baldy,' Kane calls out as he pulls away from the drive. She gives him the finger, but she's smiling.

Kane is quiet as he drives toward our street. I'm seeing him with new eyes. He's always been a great friend, but I've been so caught up in myself that I hadn't noticed he was going through stuff of his own, just like Shell. Well, similar but different.

'You *are* more than just a meathead, you know.'

He doesn't take his eyes off the road, but he smiles a little.

I get him to drop me off a little down the road from my house. I'm not ready just yet. We say our goodbyes and I find myself walking around the neighbourhood at dusk, watching people gardening, kids running along the footpath, families piling into cars. These people, they seem to move in the world differently, with confidence, knowing who they are and where they belong. I've never fit in. And now, with all this, I feel completely untethered. Time to yank that curtain I used to think was between me and the world away completely.

I stop in the little park near the railway line and look up at the peppercorn trees. I think about all those years with Mum and Dad, and Kane's family next door, and Shell more recently, and the swimming pool, and McDonald's – all the corners of my life as I knew it.

It was a good life, and I blew it up. I don't know what's left.

And I keep wondering, was I stolen or saved?

\* \* \*

I step through the front door of my house, dropping my backpack down in the hall before heading into the lounge. Sure enough, Mum's sitting on the sofa, downing a glass of white wine.

The most shocking thing is that the place is a mess. I've only been gone a few days but her rigid sense of order is gone. There's glasses and mugs and papers everywhere. Usually her obsessive cleaning means that you could do brain surgery on the kitchen floor. But no more.

The bottle beside her is half-empty. She looks half-empty too.

'Oh my God, you're back,' she says, jumping up awkwardly, hands flailing. She's tipsy.

'Yes.' I back away from her, hesitant.

'I've been worried sick.'

I believe her. She's a mess. Hair everywhere, dark eyes, stained shirt. No pressure stockings on. Fragile. Shaky.

What have I done to her?

'I guess you know already that we didn't go camping.'

She stares at me, her eyes as big as the rest of her is small.

'Please don't be angry with Kane, Fiona and I made him do it. I was so worried about you, especially after I found the timeline behind the wardrobe,' she says, almost under her breath. 'And we see each other a bit at physio, so he trusts me.'

'More than I can trust you, clearly.'

She sinks back onto the couch like a deflated balloon.

I pace around the room, looking at everything as if through new eyes. 'It's been a busy few days. I went to Bellanta and solved a cold case. I found out who I really am, and that Dad was actually my kidnapper. And that my real mum was a dealer who has disappeared.'

Mum sinks even further into the couch.

I'm getting worked up now. 'And now I want to know what *you* know about this. You and Dad kept this secret for years!' I yell.

She nods, a small jerk. 'Yes. There's no excuse, but we did.' She pushes her hair off her forehead. 'Come Gussy, sit down and I'll explain it all.'

'Did Kane tell you I met the Crales? That they drugged me and took me into the cellar where they kept me all those years ago?'

She takes in a sharp breath. 'Oh Gus . . . I . . . I—' Her hands cover her mouth in shock.

'Don't you mean Robin? Gus doesn't really exist, does he?'

She shakes her head. 'Of course Gus exists. *You* exist. And I am still your mother.'

'Are you though?'

I sit down on the chair opposite her, watching her like she's a snake about to strike.

She stares into her glass, swirling the wine around.

'Okay. I'll tell you everything from the beginning. I met Tom Green and his young son Angus here in Melbourne when you were about three. He told me he was a single parent, but he never said much about your mother at first, just that she had taken off. You were skinny and barely speaking, but I fell in love with both of you very quickly. But frankly, I knew there was an odd streak in him, even then.'

'What do you mean?'

'He would act . . . questionably. He used to buy things like camera gear, get the receipts, then ring the police saying he was robbed to get the money back on insurance. I didn't find out the truth about you for years. I promise I didn't. And when I did find out, before I even had time to process it, we had the car accident. I didn't want to lose you, so, to my eternal shame, I kept my mouth shut. I'll never forgive myself for that.'

'How could you keep that a secret for five years?'

She raises her glass of wine toward me. 'This is my daily guilt minimiser.'

I shake my head.

She continues. 'He never told me all the details. He thought it was safer if I never knew everything, but I knew enough. He did a terrible thing, and he got away with it.'

I touch the marks on my arm, still a little warm.

She watches my hand, her grip on her glass tightening, like it's a lit firecracker she's about to throw into the air. 'Did you find out about them too?'

I nod.

'When he told me about them, I was angry with her . . . with Jane . . . for letting that happen to you.' She tosses her pack of smokes to the floor with disgust.

'He told me they were birthmarks.'

She quickly wipes away the tears forming in her eyes. 'He didn't know what else to tell you. You didn't seem to remember anything from back then. Like your first three years were just wiped from your memory. Dr Yamada said that's not uncommon for young kids who've experienced trauma.'

'So Dad saw some burn marks and took me, just like that?'

'You were being *hurt*!' she cries. I jump at the pain in her voice. It's not wailing like when her legs are giving her grief. This is different. It's guttural. Her tears flow freely.

'You were a beautiful boy who deserved love and to be looked after. In Tom's mind, he was saving you, protecting you. And since he's been gone, I've tried to do the same.'

'Is that why you've been treating me like a little kid since he died?'

'I'm sorry. Ever since the accident, I'm just so scared of . . . everything. It's been hard, keeping this secret. Loving you but fearing that you could be taken away one day.'

'Both of you kept me from Jane.'

Part of me is angry, part of me is sad.

I remember what Firelli said about a paper trail. 'How about my birth certificate?'

She looks into her hands. 'I lied to you. You do have a birth certificate, but it's fake. Someone Tom knew from his days in and out of foster homes forged one for you and him. It cost $500. How odd, the things you remember.'

'How come you were arguing a lot before he died? Why were you drunk down the tunnels that time?'

She puts her glass down on the coffee table and rubs the back of her neck with both hands.

'That was the day he told me the truth. I wanted to tell you, but he insisted we stay quiet. Then we had the accident and I was too afraid to tell you, since you'd just lost your dad.'

'Once he died you should have just told me.'

'Oh Gussy, I thought about it *every day*. But I wanted you to have nice memories of him and I was afraid of what you'd do if you knew the truth, and . . .' she pauses and wipes her eyes. 'I know what he did is unthinkable. But you were in danger, *real danger*. You have to forgive him. And I hope you can forgive me one day for covering it up.'

Suddenly I remember what she said to Dad the day he died. 'That last day with him at the hospital, why did you ask him for forgiveness? I thought it was for kidnapping me, but that can't be right, can it?'

'Oh, that. I was asking him for forgiveness for the car accident. It was my fault, Gussy.'

I'm shaking. 'You mean Robin?'

'No, you are Angus. Robin was a hurt little boy who was in danger. You are a strong young man.'

I'd give anything to talk to Dr Yamada right now. I am all over the place. 'It's too late anyway. Detective Sergeant Firelli from Bellanta arrested the Crales. They've confessed. Firelli knows everything.'

'Everything?'

I nod.

Silently, she gets her mobile phone from her handbag on the floor and stabs in a number. 'I think it's time I spoke to the police,' she says, looking me right in the eye.

I grab the phone out of her hands, cancelling the call. 'No!' I yelp.

'Angus, what's left to do but for me to confess?'

'Firelli said that if you confess, you could be charged with withholding information about a crime. Even if you get put on a good behaviour bond, they'll still take me and put me into foster care till I'm eighteen.'

There's real pain in her eyes. 'I don't want you to be taken away. That's the last thing Tom would have wanted too. But I don't know what else to do to make up for this.'

I don't know either. 'Let's call Firelli and see what he thinks.' I grab my phone and call him, putting him on speaker and setting my phone down on the coffee table.

He answers, and after I explain what's happened, and that Mum is here, I ask what has happened with the Crales.

'Mrs Crale has confessed to everything. It seems clear that Mr Crale was an accessory after the fact. Mrs Crale will be charged with kidnapping. But given her age and her terminal cancer, she'll be bailed pending further investigation.'

'Will she go to prison?' I ask.

'She may end up in a psychiatric facility. As we say in the force, the question is usually "mad or bad?" With her I think it's both.'

Mum looks at me, acceptance on her face. 'Detective Firelli, it's Meg Green here. Gus's mum. Five years ago I found out the truth about Tom – sorry, Mark – and how he came to have Gus. He never told me all of the details, but I kept what I did know to myself. Something I am ashamed about.'

There's silence at the other end.

She continues with the story in full, with me adding bits along the way.

'Is there any need to mention Mum in all of this? You have your kidnapper now, and their accomplice. Is there any need for Mum to tell the police that she knew?'

There's a cough on the other end of the line. 'Off the record, Mrs Green, if you make a statement, Gus may be taken off you and put into care.'

'Okay,' says Mum shakily.

Firelli adds, 'You will be interviewed about Reynolds at some stage. Just say you didn't know about Gus's origins and stick to that story. He's already been taken away from his family once, I don't think it should happen again.'

Mum lets out a deep sigh. 'I . . . thank you, so much.'

He lets out a chuckle. 'You've got a good kid, Mrs Green. He'll make a good cop one day.'

I hang up, beaming. Mum reaches for my hand. 'Everything will be fine,' she says in a quiet, wobbly voice. I'm not sure if she's talking to me or herself. 'I'm so glad you're home now.'

There's so many things we have to say. But right now, sitting here with her is enough.

# Chapter 33

# Fishtank

The next few days and weeks are a planet-sized blur of noise all mushed together in the blender in my head. Memories swirl in and out as I struggle to work out what order they happened in.

The big thing is the media. Once the Crales were formally charged, and the story broke, there were journalists everywhere. It may have been a New South Wales story, but there was national interest. Not many kidnap cases ultimately have a happy ending, so reporters from Victoria and New South Wales have latched onto my story. Mum is refusing all interviews, supported by the police, who are still investigating some aspects of the case.

With everything that's been going on, I haven't had to go back to school. I had to have a meeting with Mum and the school principal, along with the school counsellor and the year nine coordinator. All these people in a room, talking about my options. They're going to use marks I already have to assess me, and not make me sit exams. Big relief. I can barely focus on breakfast these days, let alone study for an exam.

It all happened after hours so I didn't have to interact with other students. Kane makes out like they put a hood over my head and smuggled me into school undercover like a pop star or a mafia kingpin. They didn't, but his version is more fun.

I've had to delete my socials. It all went a bit crazy for the first few days, with lots of messages from people who had never bothered to ever speak to me before. And trolls shit-posting, which is just weird.

I had hoped that all this media coverage would lead to Jane contacting me, or that someone would come forward with information about her – but nothing yet.

I did text Anna and told her about Robin being in a cellar nearby. I told her to contact the *Courier* and make sure they run a piece about how she was right after all.

Sophie's been in constant contact. She wants to come visit me some time, but I put her off. I'm getting to see that clingy side of her that people mentioned.

* * *

The main thing I did in those first few days was go and see Dr Yamada.

He's got this strange office off a manky laneway in the city. Dark red walls, dark brown wooden reception desk, and an enormous plastic fern in the corner, covered in dust. The receptionist is about a thousand years old and looks like she's covered in dust too. As always, she asks my name as if she's never seen me before.

Every time I have an appointment I am mesmerised by the giant fish tank in the waiting room. It's huge, like two metres long, and built into the wall. Watching the fish swim about is calming. Their world is small and finite and knowable – I envy them that right now.

Eventually Dr Yamada sticks his head out the door. 'Angus?' he calls, smiling. He's a Japanese guy with vivid eyes and a calm face. He's wearing a green Hawaiian shirt today. He seems to have a collection of them. They used to annoy me at first, but now I find them reassuring.

His office is lighter than reception. There's a long vertical window set high up on one wall, which brings in a lot of light. The walls are cream and there's plants everywhere, from pots in the corner to some hanging from his bookshelf.

I remember the first time I came here I had to put my hands on my knees to stop my legs from shaking. I was worried that if I looked nervous then he'd think I had something to hide. I remember staring at the plants instead of his face. It was only after a few visits that I realised they were fake.

Dr Yamada sits back in his chair and points me to the chair opposite him. 'So, it's been a big few days. Life-changing. Traumatic. How are you coping?'

'I'm okay. I can't sleep at night but it's all I want to do during the day. I might start swimming again. You can't really think too much when you're underwater.'

'That sounds like a nice idea. Now, why don't we start at the beginning? Tell me what's happened in the last few days. Tell me about Robin.'

Dr Yamada waits for me to talk. It's not like therapy on TV. It's confronting and awkward. Particularly today.

When I start summing everything up line by line, it sounds like a bad TV episode.

'Robin was neglected by his drug-dealing mother and possibly abused. He was kidnapped, indirectly, by his mother's ex, and kept in a cellar by the neighbour over the road. Eventually he was taken to Melbourne by his kidnapper, who he thought was his father, and raised there with his kidnapper's new girlfriend, who he thought was his actual mother. When he grew up he did some investigating into his past and dug up secrets that ended him up in the same cellar again. He nearly drowned escaping.'

'There's a lot to unpack there,' Dr Yamada says. *Argh, he always says that.*

'First up, you seem a bit disconnected from it. It's like you're telling me about a movie you saw, not about your own experience.'

I shrug. 'It feels like a movie sometimes, like it's too crazy to be real. Am I allowed to say crazy in here?'

He smiles. 'Yes, you're allowed to say that. Now, let's start with some questions.'

I realise I am bracing myself in my seat, arms gripping the chair, feet pushed hard to the floor. It's like I'm on a rollercoaster at Luna Park.

He spins his pen around in his hand, finger to finger. 'Tell me how you feel about Robin.'

I look at the certificates on the wall. Does three certificates mean he has three degrees? 'I don't know,' I reply, avoiding his eyes.

'Do you think he is strong?'

'Yes.'

'Stronger than you?

'Maybe.' Funny how the carpet seems a different colour today, greyer.

'Because he survived all these things?'

'Yes.' There's a half-eaten apple sitting on his desk.

'Do you believe in fate?'

My arms relax a little. The abstract questions are easier. 'Kinda. Everyone gets a bucket of good luck and a bucket of bad.'

Dr Yamada taps his pen on his pad three times. 'Do you think it was fate that Robin was kidnapped?'

Feet hard to the floor again. 'I don't know.'

Dr Yamada just smiles patiently at me. I find myself filling the silence again. 'I mean I guess it was, but I don't see what the point was. Like if fate is a big grand plan or whatever, then I don't see how this fits in.'

Dr Yamada leans in closer. 'What if fate doesn't exist – and I'm not saying it doesn't – what then? Why do bad things happen to good people? What if there is no reason, only the here and now?'

'Then we're all doomed I guess,' I joke. But it's a spooky thought.

'What about Robin, does he believe in fate?'

Fingers gripping. 'I'm not sure.'

Dr Yamada uncrosses and recrosses his legs slowly. 'Why don't you ask him?'

This is getting really weird. I scratch my stomach. 'How do you mean?'

'I want you to ask Robin if he believes in fate or not.'

I look up at him, confused. 'I can't.'

Dr Yamada taps his pen on his palm. 'Why not?'

Arms burning, feet aching. 'I just can't.'

'Come on Gus, why?' he asks softly.

I take a breath. How do I answer this? 'He's like, part of me, but not me at the same time.'

'Can you expand on that a bit more?'

'I can't. Can we talk about something else?'

Dr Yamada sits back in his chair and scribbles a lot of notes. Bloody hell, what is he writing? He doesn't usually take this many notes when we talk.

'What else would you like to talk about?'

'Dunno.'

'Okay. Tell me, when you found out more information about Robin, and the case, how did you feel?'

'Confused. And angry. Dad and the Crales ruined my life and Mum covered it up.'

'When you say they ruined your life, can you explain how?'

My arms are crossed now. I'm getting really shitty with him. 'Well, to start with, my whole life is just a bag of lies.'

'I appreciate that.'

I'm furious now. 'Dad and the Crales stole me from my real mother! Dad changed my name, hid my real identity. And Mum kept his secret.'

'But they loved you and you loved them?'

'I guess, but—'

'It's okay to be angry with them and still love them.'

It's too much. I start to cry. I was totally not going to do this in front of him today.

Dr Yamada makes a soft, reassuring noise. 'It's okay to feel confused. I just want you to connect to your feelings on this. But you do have to think more about Robin and you being one and the same, not separate. Try to think of it as gaining a friend rather than losing yourself.'

This sounds nuts but also kind of makes sense.

'How much control do you feel you have at the moment? Are you taking your meds? Are you cutting?' he asks.

This time I look him right in the eye. 'Some. Yes. No cutting.'

'Good,' he says, smiling.

\* \* \*

Later on, as I step out into the daylight of the alley, I feel a bit better. The hot air hits me, bouncing off the brown bricks and metal bins. I squint up into the light. I don't know how Robin and I fit together either yet, but it feels like a start.

Mum's waiting for me in the cafe round the corner. She doesn't ask me what I talk to Dr Yamada about. There's this whirlwind around us, so it feels really important to just talk about ordinary things like driving lessons and joining the police one day.

When she said Dad saved me . . . did he? Maybe Jane would have eventually stopped dealing to be a proper mother to me. Maybe she would have gotten a job and we would have had a nice little life together, just the two of us. Maybe she would have met a nice guy and I would have been part of a normal family.

Or maybe it all would have gotten worse and I would have ended up in care, just as Dad (I can't bring myself to call him Mark) feared? Maybe I would have had a shit time of it like he did?

Like she can read my mind, Mum leans in and touches my face. 'Everything will be okay Angus. We'll get through this. The media frenzy will die down. The investigation will end. You'll go back to school next year. I'll still be here. And I'll do all I can to make it up to you – for everything.'

The fishhooks are gone.

# Chapter 34

# Sledgehammer

I'm with Shell, leaning on my front fence. As she runs her hand through her growing-back hair, it flickers in the light. I'm more conscious of my own messy hair now that hers is so slick.

I see that she is changing. Not just the hair and the clothes, but everything. She seems to be confident again, like she used to be, but even more so if that's possible. Like she's standing a little taller or something, filling out the space she was always meant to take up.

'C'mon, tell me everything,' I say.

'Well, I sat them down and told them I had something important to discuss. Cheryl kept getting up to fuss over something on the stove, deflecting, but I told her to sit,' she says.

'And? What did you say? How did it go? Give me details!'

'The same thing I told you, about not feeling very "me". About feeling more like a girl some days, more like something else other days, but not in a fixed way. Cheryl freaked out, and gasped like she heard a gunshot. But I think it was a generic reaction to things not being the way she likes or expects.'

'I can imagine that.'

'She asked me a few questions, like if I feel more like a girl than a boy, like she needs a percentage. And then Larry asked if there are certain things that make me feel unsure, like it's a food allergy!'

'Are you allergic to being a girl?' I joke.

'No, just allergic to you,' she laughs. 'Cheryl and Larry will be fine. They just don't understand yet. I mean, I barely do, so . . .'

'That makes sense.' I reach out and squeeze her hand.

Kane turns up and plonks himself between us. 'Goose, what name are you gonna use now? Robgus? Gusbin?' he says, pissing himself laughing.

'I'm keeping Gus.'

He turns to Shell. 'What about you, you gonna change your name? Michelle is quite a whaddyacallit . . . gendered name?'

'I like Shell. That name's not about gender. It's about how tough I am.'

She is tough. She has been amazing these last few days. Both of them have. I don't know what I'd do without them.

Kane jumps to his feet. 'Look at you two, all feelings and transformations. It's like one of those shitty teen shows you watch.'

I snicker. 'What about you? You and your "I'm more than a set of muscles"?'

Kane cracks his knuckles. Shell and I shudder at the sound.

'Yeah, whatever. Are you ready to do this?'

'Yes.' I say.

'What did he need this for anyway?' Shell asks in Dad's shed, lifting the sledgehammer onto her shoulder like she's a lumberjack.

'Who knows? The shed is full of crap he bought but never used. He was a Bunnings addict.'

We walk down to the back of my yard where the cubbyhouse sits like a cancer.

'Ready?' Kane asks.

'A hundred per cent,' I say. I hand him my phone.

'Why are you filming this?' Shell asks.

'Dr Yamada said it might be cathartic to watch it later.'

She nods, semi-convinced, handing me the sledgehammer. It's so heavy I nearly drop it.

Kane points the phone at me. 'Action.'

The feel of the sledgehammer's weight as it slams against the door is powerful. I never dreamed something could be so satisfying. I have a lot of feelings swirling around inside of me and it's good to tear into something so physically. This is what cutting used to feel like. As the glass in the windows break with a discordant smash, I half expect to see the ghost of past me float by.

Within ten minutes the little hut is decimated, a pile of wood and glass and bad memories. It was quite easy to demolish. Dad wasn't good at building. Still, I wonder what Mum will think when she gets home?

'Are you going to recycle this wood and glass?' Shell asks. I'm not sure if she's serious or not.

'That's a wrap,' says Kane, handing me my phone back.

And it is. The end of the thing and the beginning of other things.

I feel like we need to celebrate somehow. 'Let's go to Luna Park! Let's have a *Love, Simon* moment.'

\* \* \*

Walking through the bright red gaping clown mouth at Luna Park never gets old. It's like a time machine. Whatever age you are, once you walk through those gates, it's like you're a kid the world is opening out its arms to. I think Mum first brought me here when I was about seven. I remember the fear and the thrill of the rides, and vomiting up pink goo that was once fairy floss after the dodgem cars. Still, it was a good day.

'Dagwood dog?' Shell asks, pointing to the deep-fried battered hotdogs on a stick. Who came up with that?

'You know it's not food at all, right?' scoffs Kane.

I shake my head and point to the fairy floss.

She smirks. 'You are peak gay today.'

We sit on a bench near the dodgem cars and eat while Kane wanders around, listening to the buzzing sound of the static electricity burning the air. The weird sauce that comes with the dagwood dog is all over Shell's face and I have pink bristles coating my lips.

The air is filled with the screams of thrilled children and adults as they ride the terrifying G-force ride. There's no way I would get on that. A million miles in the air and then you just drop? Never.

'Want to give it a try?' asks Kane, slapping my shoulder.

I shake my head. Shell snorts. 'As if.'

He shrugs and marches off.

Shell stands up and grabs my hand. 'Ferris wheel?'

'Yep.'

We stand in the queue of kids unashamedly, towering over them like those Easter Island statues. When we get to the front of the line, the operator guy looks us up and down. 'We'll fit,' Shell says to him, death stare daring him to disagree, and barges to the carriage. I follow and we squeeze in together – and I do mean squeeze – it's a tight fit. But we do it. We pull the safety bar down, wedged together within a Perspex and metal cage.

'So, still no word from Jane?'

'The police still haven't found her. But I reckon she's still out there, somewhere. If she was dead, it'd be easier to trace her, right?'

Shell nods. 'All this media attention should help.'

The story is getting so much coverage, especially in New South Wales. I don't understand how she can't have come forward by now.

'Just leaves one question unanswered though, doesn't it?' says Shell.

'The website?'

She nods.

'Yeah, the police haven't been able to trace who put that ad up. It might have been Jane, but it could be someone else entirely. I may never know.'

'Still, it's been fun playing detective.'

'It doesn't have to end. We could start a detective agency. Say it's for that Business Studies assignment, but it'll really be for us,' I say.

Her big eyes light up like its Christmas. 'Yes, let's do it. We'd be brilliant.'

The magical sing-song carnival music kicks in and swirls around us. The carriage jolts into action and we rise up into the sky.

# Acknowledgements

When I was a kid, I would obsessively read C.S Lewis, Terrance Dicks, and Agatha Christie, dreaming that one day I might write a book too. Becoming a published author would have remained a dream if not for a village of talented and kind people who helped me along the way.

To begin at the end, big thanks to Wakefield Press, Michael Bollen, and Maddy Sexton for agreeing to publish this book. Thanks to Jo Case for giving me pages of positive feedback, to Maddy Sexton for being an amazing and supportive editor, to Polly Grant Butler for publicity expertise, and to Josh Durham for his fantastic cover design. You all helped make this writing dream come true.

Thanks to Hachette and the Queensland Writers Centre for choosing me to participate in their 2019 Manuscript Development Program. That's where I met my future agent, the very cool and wise Jane Novak. Thanks Jane for finding a home for Gus.

Kate Belle, Michael Earp, Tracey Foster, Nicole Hayes, Imbi Neeme, and Sydney Smith each looked at this manuscript at different times, providing excellent, encouraging advice, so thanks so much to you all. Thanks also to great YA writers Amy Kaufman and Holden Sheppard who shared their time and wisdom with me.

At Writers Victoria I completed two writing courses that helped me understand how to shape a book, thanks to Andrea Goldsmith

(2010) and Antoni Jach (2016). Not only were these courses insightful, but I became mates with other attendees and we ended up forming two amazing writing groups at different times: 'The Little Lonsdale Group' (Joanne Baker, Jewelene Barrile, Kate Belle, Leslie Falkiner-Rose, Kathryn Ledson, Margareta Osborn, Jennifer Scoullar, Dianne Simonelli and Anja Tanhane), and 'The Prologues' (Deborah Crabtree, Karen McKnight, Imbi Neeme, Edwina Preston, and Clive Wansbrough). If my writing is any good, it's because you people taught me how.

I also couldn't have completed this book without some expert advice from Kate Ursprung for all things medical, Adam [Redacted] for police procedural advice, and some folk who wish to remain anonymous for sharing their experiences with anxiety and self-harm.

I'm also lucky enough to have a group of friends I've known most of my life, who have spent decades listening to me droning on about writing a book and yet kept encouraging me: Pauline Basilio, Ross Carland, Jennifer Castles, the late Peter Couttas, Robert Diedrich, Dietrich Hausler, Mel Hosemans, Lorelle Martin, Kerri McCormack, Andrea McNamara, Sara McQueenie, Cory Parfett, Adam Richard, Deb Stokes, and Kate Ursprung.

I was raised by my grandparents so I wish Ira and Stan Hunter were still around so I could say thanks to them – I think they'd be quite proud. I know my mother Kay would be, if she was still here. Thanks to the rest of my family – Bianca, Guy, and Peter – for putting up with me all these years.

Last, but never least, thanks to my partner Dean Walliss for reading drafts, listening to ideas, and always making space in our lives for my writing.

And ultimately, THANK YOU for buying or borrowing this book. It means everything to me.

Having a tough time and need someone to talk to right now?
The following services are there to listen and help you out.
They are confidential and available 24/7.

### Kids Helpline

1800 551 800

www.kidshelpline.com.au

### headspace

1800 650 890

www.headspace.org.au

### Beyond Blue

1300 224 636

beyondblue.com.au

Wakefield Press is an independent publishing and
distribution company based in Adelaide, South Australia.
We love good stories and publish beautiful books.
To see our full range of books, please visit our website at
www.wakefieldpress.com.au
where all titles are available for purchase.
To keep up with our latest releases and news,
subscribe to the Wakefield Weekly at
https://mailchi.mp/wakefieldpress/subscribe

Find us!

Facebook: www.facebook.com/wakefield.press
Instagram: www.instagram.com/wakefieldpress

www.ingramcontent.com/pod-product-compliance
Lightning Source LLC
Chambersburg PA
CBHW020559030726
47497CB00007B/2009